P9-CCV-230

Hoofbeats

Lara and the Gray Mare

Book One

by KATHLEEN DUEY

DUTTON CHILDREN'S BOOKS
NEW YORK

DUTTON CHILDREN'S BOOKS
A division of Penguin Young Readers Group

Published by the Penguin Group
Penguin Young Readers Group, 345 Hudson Street,
New York, New York 10014, U.S.A.
Penguin Group (Canada), 10 Alcorn Avenue, Toronto, Ontario,
Canada M4V 3B2 (a division of Pearson Penguin Canada Inc.)
Penguin Books Ltd, 80 Strand, London WC2R 0RL, England
Penguin Ireland, 25 St Stephen's Green, Dublin 2, Ireland
(a division of Penguin Books Ltd)
Penguin Group (Australia), 250 Camberwell Road, Camberwell,
Victoria 3124, Australia (a division of Pearson Australia Group Pty Ltd)
Penguin Books India Pvt Ltd, 11 Community Centre,
Panchsheel Park, New Delhi - 110 017, India
Penguin Group (NZ), Cnr Airborne and Rosedale Roads, Albany,
Auckland 1310, New Zealand (a division of Pearson New Zealand Ltd)
Penguin Books (South Africa) (Pty) Ltd, 24 Sturdee Avenue,
Rosebank, Johannesburg 2196, South Africa

Penguin Books Ltd, Registered Offices: 80 Strand,
London WC2R 0RL, England

LIBRARY OF CONGRESS CATALOGING-IN-PUBLICATION DATA

Duey, Kathleen.
Lara and the gray mare / by Kathleen Duey.
p. cm. — (Hoofbeats ; bk. 1)
Summary: While her father is away fighting the Normans and other
Irish clans, nine-year-old Lara works hard to help harvest food
and also helps care for the pregnant gray mare that she loves.
ISBN: 0-525-47332-7
[1. Horses—Fiction. 2. Ireland—History—Fiction.] I. Title.
PZ7.D8694Lar 2005
[Fic]—dc22
2004053521

Published simultaneously by Dutton Children's Books and Puffin Books,
divisions of Penguin Young Readers Group
345 Hudson Street, New York, New York 10014
www.penguin.com/youngreaders

Printed in USA · First Edition

1 3 5 7 9 10 8 6 4 2

For Star, a dapple gray Welsh Pony, with a true, five-point white star on his side. He was the smartest pony I have ever known. I met him in a dark pasture, in a driving rain, on the night he was born. Birth is a fierce, joyous miracle. Anyone who falls in love with a newborn foal is permanently touched, forever changed, forever grateful.

CHAPTER ONE

✿ ✿ ✿

The girl who comes to stand beside me in the early
mornings brings me handfuls of barley—and her soft voice.
I am so glad to be away from shouting men
and the barbed scents of anger and blood.

"Larach!" Fallon cried out in the dusk before the sunrise. "Lara O'Marchach!"

Her voice was loud enough to wake a rock.

Of course I did not answer her.

I am no fool. And I was on my way to see if the gray mare had foaled. So I skittered to the side, silent as a night breeze, and I hid in the black shadows beneath the old oak that stands beside the gates.

Fallon is my aunt, now fourteen years old and not yet married.

She is five years older than I am, and she scares me. Her voice is as shrill as iron on stone, hard put.

I can tell you true that I have been afraid of Fallon all my life because she has always been mean to me. She was mean to my brothers, too, when they were little. Do I need more reasons to dread her? You may add this to the count, then: Until I was old enough to outwit her, she often stole my supper and lied about it. She still takes more than her share sometimes.

At sunset, just as the new day is beginning, Fallon likes to stand out where she can see the distant shine of the sea, her hands on her hips. She'd pick a fight with nightfall if she could. She is, after all, my father's little sister. They share the same temper.

My mother says Father is a calmer man now at twenty-nine than he was at sixteen when they married. He is both loved and feared by all our relatives, all the people in our tuath.

And by me.

My grandfather was only feared, the old ones say, so I suppose we O'Marchachs are improving with time.

"Lara?"

Ah. Fallon had made her voice gentler, but I was not taken in by that. I ducked farther back into the slanting branches of the oak. Fallon knew where to look for me this early. I always went to talk to the gray mare. She was entirely healed now. It had taken a long time.

The gray was a beauty, taller and more graceful than any horse I had ever seen. My father had found her grazing free on his last journey, wearing a bridle with a broken throat latch and dragging one rein, a wound on her foreleg. There was a burn mark on her jaw, a strange design that could not have been an accident. What tuath marked their horses with fire scars?

Some battle had freed the gray from her owner, my father guessed. He had brought her limping home, and I had nursed her every day, bringing lichen and cress to stanch the wound until it healed.

That was when my visits to the gray mare began.

I could not take time from my work, so I slept less, creeping out of the house to go stand beside her in the dark, talking quietly so she would know that she was not alone. It raised her spirits, I could tell. She began eating better and she healed.

My father had never thanked me for nursing her back to soundness. But he had been happy to hear she was in foal. When I realized it, I had been dizzy with joy.

Girls are not allowed to have horses. But since I had saved the mare, had cared for her so well, I hoped my father would consider giving the foal to me. When he came home from whatever battle he was fighting now, I intended to try to talk him into it.

"Lara!"

Fallon's shout shattered my thoughts and I held still as a rabbit beside a wolf path as she passed before me and opened the gates to go into the rath. She called my name three more times inside, then came out again.

I could hear the mares shifting uneasily as they stood inside the great circle of the earthen walls, startled by the intrusion. I recognized the high, gentle neigh of the gray mare. If Fallon didn't give up, I would have to go to my day's work without seeing the mare.

I let out a long breath as Fallon came back past me and headed for our cottage. I knew why she was angry, and there was nothing I could do about it. I pressed my back against the outer earthen wall and tried to decide what to do. I wanted so much to go see the gray mare, but I was afraid Fallon would come back and find me there, inside the rath.

The walls of the rath are simply this: monstrous big heaps of earth, shaped like giant rings, one inside the other, both broken for two carts' width at one place, to let people pass in and out. That's where the gates are.

We keep the mares inside the earthen walls at night. During the day, boys herd them out to graze. They won't let me help. I am not a boy.

My father says it is a rare thing for a rath to have *two* earthen walls. Usually there is only one. He has traveled near to Dublin and back and has seen only one other like ours. Perhaps the ones who built it so long ago had better harvests than others did. Maybe they had the strength to keep digging and dirt piling for years.

Inside the huge earthen walls, the ground is

open except for four little round byres that my father says were once houses. Now the stock uses them for shelter in the rain.

I shivered and pulled my woolen brat closer around my shoulders and tugged the thick cloth down to cover my arms. The brown wool was softened with wear. We were finally past the last cold days of Gam. I could not wait to see the sun after all the dreary days of people and animals wet and trembling with cold.

Fallon did not call my name again for such a long time that I dared hope, even though I know her too well, that she might have given up. A moment passed, then two. The silence was lovely, lovely, and the morning sky was passing from deep gray to lighter gray. But I was not fooled. I knew she was trying to trick me into coming out if I was hiding.

So I did not.

I looked up at the gray sky instead. The day before had been sunny and fine, and I hoped this would be another cloudless day. I had not pondered long on the graying sky before I heard tiptoe footsteps on the path. Fallon was coming back. I knelt down, then stayed perfectly still.

Fallon passed—I could see her easily now in the dawn dusk. She went on around the rath, following the curve of the outer earth wall until she struck off toward the stream. Then she began shouting again. I could hear her all the way down to the cows; then the direction of her voice changed, and I knew she was headed back again.

She had probably gone just far enough to see that there were no candles lit in the dairy byre, that I was not starting my day's work early. Bebinn, Gerroc, and I were always up before most of the others because we had to milk. It didn't take that long this time of year. The few cows that had been bred late enough to have winter calves were drying up, giving less and less milk every day. And they were so tame we didn't even have to put spancels on their front legs to hold them still.

Work of all kinds is lightened by Bebinn and Gerroc. We are like sisters, we are so close in age.

"LARA!"

The shout made me shudder. Fallon was on her way back up the hill. I knew exactly why she was so angry with me. It was this simple: She had, after five days, decided to comb her knotted hair.

Magnus had not meant to ruin Fallon's carved antler comb, but he had. He was my littlest cousin; he was Gerroc's youngest brother.

Magnus had played with the comb five days past without asking, and he had dropped it where one of the dogs could snatch it up and run. By the time he had gotten it back, the comb was cracked.

Any dog will chew bone, of course. It is their instinct and their right. How was the hound to know that this bit of antler had been carefully sawed and that the row of slender close-set teeth would be so fragile?

Unfortunately, this was no ordinary comb. It had belonged to my grandmother—Fallon's and my father's mother. It had been given to Fallon on my grandmother's death, when Fallon had been barely old enough to use it without help.

I knew she cherished it.

I knew she prized that comb more than she cared for whoever had caused the damage, plain and simple. Magnus knew it, too.

It was I, coming back from evening milking,

who found Magnus crying behind the offal heap
near the grain fields. The new-hatched spring
flies were buzzing around the rotting manure and
the piles of last year's cornstalks. The ruined
comb was tight in his little hands.

I could not think what else to do, so we washed
it carefully and put it back in Fallon's wooden
box. I hoped she might think she had cracked it
herself without knowing. Small chance—I should
have known better.

Fallon was always eager to lay blame for any
mishap upon someone else. And she had clearly
assumed the blame was mine. Ah, well. Better me
than poor little Magnus. She was in a fine temper.
Little Magnus hardly needed her to drag him
about by his ear, thumping his thin back. Not
that I would enjoy it, mind you, but I had stood
it from her before, many times, and it wasn't so
awful as it sounds. I was bigger now and she
couldn't hold on to me very long.

Little Magnus walked with a limp. He had
wandered into the cattle herd when he could
barely toddle and a cow had stepped on him. The
hurt leg had healed crooked and his gait was

changed forever. Even so, he was sunny and he worked hard and he sang like a bird. I liked him very much. Everyone did. Except Fallon. Listening to her footsteps come closer, I was hard-pressed to think of anyone she did like. I was entirely unable to think of anyone who liked *her*. Even my father—who was her very own brother—could only stand her for a while before he found some excuse to take his leave.

He said Fallon was like their father in that way—easy to anger, always ready for a fight. He had also said it was a shame she wasn't a boy, that she would have taken to sword and bow and battle like birds to the air. One thing was clear; she had never taken to spinning thread or weaving, grinding grain, making bread, or any of the work girls and women had to do day in and day out. Half the time, she had her sleeves rolled up to bare her forearms and her leine hitched up like a boy. She liked to work without the long hem shortening her stride.

This is shameful, but it is true: I prayed every evening to the old ones, the saints, and the faeries that some man would be stupid enough to marry Fallon and take her away from us one day.

I knew one thing standing there in the graying light of dawn: It wouldn't be this day. She was very close again, bellowing my name, following the curve of the rath walls back around to the gates. I stiffened. It was time to make a decision or I would be stuck here so long that Bebinn and Gerroc would come looking for me. Some days, I would have just stepped out into the gray morning light and let Fallon find me, just to have it done and over with.

This morning, for whatever reason of fate, fortune, and divine guidance, I did not. Instead, when she was still just far enough away not to see me in the shadows of the oak branches, I hitched my leine up around my waist and scrambled up the massive outer earthen wall. A second later, I was tumbling down into the deep fosse that lay between the outer wall and the inner one. I landed on my feet, then pitched sideways, falling hard on my back.

I lay there for a long moment, staring up into the sky. This place between the earthen walls, dug deep to free enough dirt to build them—this was a faerie place, everyone knew. It was dangerous to trespass where they lived.

I got up, my legs a little shaky. Then I gathered a handful of the back of my leine, pulling the cloth around my body, trying to see how badly I had dirtied it. It was my newest one, not yet outgrown. It was still loose and came nearly to my ankles, the sleeves still long enough to cover my whole arm to the fingertips.

In the dim light, I could only feel the damp and the grit. At least I had not torn it. My mother might not even notice the new stains if I wrung it out in the creek, then slid it back over my head wet and wore it long enough to dry it.

My woolen brat, pulled close around my shoulders for warmth, was only a little muddied. I had landed more where I sit than anywhere else. And my mother was no fool. She had dyed the wool of my brat a light dunny brown to match the brown linen of my leine, and both of them to match the dirt.

I pulled my leine straight and shrugged my brat higher around my shoulders, then looked around. It was very odd to stand in this gigantic trough between the two circular walls. We'd had pounding rains ten or twelve days before. The water had been running through the fosse then, fast enough to hear the trickling as it sifted into the base of the walls and drained away.

"Lara!" Fallon's shout was hoarse with fury. I flinched, even knowing that she could not see me through the high earthen wall, that she would never suspect I would brave faeries to escape her. Everyone knew stories about children disappearing in the fosse, borne off by faerie folk, lost forever.

The stories might be accurate, but this was the truth: I was by far more frightened of Fallon than of any faerie that morning.

"Lara! Where are you?"

I began to walk, silently following the inner curve of the rath, moving away from her. I slid my hand along the earthen wall, grass and moss tickling my fingers. The men of the tuath had spent part of last summer repairing the outside wall, digging out loose places and repacking the soil where the rain had weakened it. For a while the patches had been easy to see. Now, after a season of rain, green had covered them.

Green. I realized that I could see colors and knew the sun was close to rising. Fallon would need only to see me at a distance to know I had not answered her call. That would bring her to a frothing rage, I was sure. I could hear her, still, talking to the empty oak branches.

"Lara, I know you are up in that tree," she growled. "Come you down. *Now*."

Shivery and scared, I began to run, hoping she would not hear my footfalls, that she would stand talking to the empty branches long enough for me to climb over the earthworks on the opposite side. If I made it all the way around the huge circle, then over the top and on to the woods, I could hide again.

Then I would simply wait. Bebinn and Gerroc would soon come to the dairy. The other women would be about their work within an hour. If I could hide that long, Fallon would be stopped at least for the day.

She had never set upon me where anyone else could see. I thought it was because my father, after all, was our rí, the lord and king of our tuath. He was Fallon's brother, true enough, but

I was his daughter, and one of *my* brothers, some-day, would take my father's place. Fergal and Trian were fostered out now, living close to the sea with another tuath, learning trades. But they would come home once they were grown. She would not dare bully them then. Nor me.

As I ran, flying along on both hope and fear, I was beginning to smile, to believe I would escape, when my toes struck a hard edge, cool and straight—unlike rock or grass or tree wood.

I stumbled to an ungraceful halt, thinking it might be some sliver of bone—or, with astound-ing luck, a comb. My mother had found hers and it was a grand one, made from elk antler with a design of carved knots on it.

Excited, hoping that the saints or the faerie folk had pitied my thudding heart and given me a fine comb to replace Fallon's cracked one, I dug at the soil. When I had it free, I wiped the object on my woolen brat. It was not a comb.

I took in a quick breath. It was a perfect oval of gold, and within it was fastened a horse shape beaten from the same pure metal. The little gold horse was galloping, its mane and tail streaming out behind it. There was a sharpened wire folded back, hinged to the gold circle.

I stared at it, smiling at my luck. How long had it lain here? Perhaps it had belonged to an ancient queen. The little brooch was meant to be worn on a smooth linen leine or a fancy silk dress. It was a dainty ornament meant for a real nobleman's daughter, not for me. My father ruled our tuath—not dozens of tuatha, not a castle or an army of many clans. We owned nothing made of gold.

"Lara?" Fallon was not closer, but she was shouting at the oak branches now; it was light enough for her to suspect that I was not in them.

Fallon would take the golden brooch from me between one heartbeat and the next if ever she saw it. I traced the oval with my fingertip, then touched it to my lips to feel the coldness of the metal. Shivering, I pinned the brooch inside the shoulder of my woolen brat, next to my body, and clambered over the earthen wall on the far side of the keep. Then I ran for the woods.

CHAPTER TWO

❧ ❧ ❧

I am restless and I graze apart from the others when the boys come to let us out each day. I feel strange, alert. I shy at birds flying past, at bees in the grass. This must have something to do with the foal that lies inside my body.

I escaped Fallon that day by working with Bebinn and Gerroc at cleaning the little byre that holds my mother's chickens. The offal we carried down to the fallow fields, holding our noses and laughing.

Bebinn has a cloud of hair the color of iron rot. It looks like an orange halo in the right light and mats down like wet reeds when she is sweating. She must have gotten it from the faeries—the rest of us have brown hair that hangs heavily down our backs.

We sing while we work, rearranging the words of the old tunes until the older women scowl at us and click their tongues. We prank and tease and laugh out loud. Gerroc has a laugh bright enough to turn a thunderstorm aside. I am convinced that the saints, the faeries, and the old gods gave me these two to make up for giving me Fallon.

Bebinn pretended to be Saint Brigid, throwing bread to the poor, instead of a girl pitching chicken manure at bare dirt.

Gerroc laughed so hard I thought she might burst.

Bebinn can make anyone laugh.

We scattered the manure thinly where the winter wheat was growing. Later, the men would plow both wheat and offal under, churning it into the soil to rot slowly over the coming year. The fields ready for planting had been rested the same way last year.

"I wonder," I said as we trudged back up the hill, "what it would be like to have a whole year to rest."

Bebinn and Gerroc both stared at me. Then Bebinn began to smile. Gerroc caught the giggles from her, and they both laughed so hard their cheeks flushed pink. None of us could imagine it.

"We will work hard at high pasture," Bebinn said as we dragged the next load down the hill.

"How strange it will be—to be anywhere but right here," I said. Then we all fell silent and I knew they had the same mixture of excitement and fear in their bellies that I did.

ॐ ॐ ॐ

I avoided Fallon's anger that night by staying close to my mother all evening. The next morning, I pretended to sleep a little late, opening my eyes a tiny slit, watching Fallon frown at me, with dark eyes and a wrinkled brow, as she left.

I rose once she was gone, my stomach cramped with hunger. It was like this nearly every morning, and I knew that was part of Fallon's temper fits over her cracked comb. She was hungry most the time. We all were. None among us ever had enough to eat this season of the year, and it would only get worse before it got better.

From Imbolc, on the first of February, to Beltaine on the first day of May, we were caught between the end of our winter stores and the beginning of our new food. Lambing began earlier than calving and that meant the sheep would give milk, but it would be much less than the cows would later.

Some years were worse than others, and this was a bad one. My father had been gone most of last summer fighting, then had left again not long after our celebration of Imbolc and the passing of Saint Brigid through the tuath.

You could not see her, of course, it was her spirit—but we left out things for her to bless. My mother had left out her biggest iron soup pot, as she always does. I put out my spindle, hoping it would spin faster so I could spend less time at a chore I hated.

After my father left, and all his men with him, we had only a few aged men and the young boys to hunt for us. So meat was scarce and we dared not kill many cows without my father's command. Once the two-year bulls were gone, we lived on last year's oats and hard cheese. There wasn't much. As the days passed, all our bellies got flatter, curving in instead of out.

We had not been the only ones to eat our food, of course. The tuath had paid shares of cheese and grain and meat to my father so that he could pay the Norman barony of Athenry. Until the Irishmen defeated the Normans—if they ever did—we would have to pay them.

And all through the wet, wintry months of Gam, we had to receive noble visitors if they came to us. We had had quite a few this year—Lord Birmingham, the Norman Baron of Athenry, had sent us two groups of young noblemen off to explore the wild lands of Connemara. I wondered if any of them would end up fighting against my father if the battling continued once the weather warmed again. I wondered if any of them knew which tuatha fought and which had accepted their rule.

The first of the Normans had stayed with us for two days on their way west, resting their horses and eating and asking all manner of questions about the deer in the forest and whether we used seaweed in our fields and so on.

They had stopped to stay with us again coming home, eating heartily of our cheese and apples and meat, refusing pea soup and asking for more mead until they dozed at the table. The second group had eaten as much and had been less interested in anything we had to say.

Then, a month after the feast day of Imbolc, when the weather was just starting to warm a little, three of them had come back. This time they brought two priests who wanted to talk to my father. He had not been home, of course, and the old men had given the priests a story about my father being off hunting. The Normans had brought a spare horse and loaded it with our food for the clergymen.

The visitors had all been a marvel to watch. I loved looking at the fineness of their clothes, the wrought gold and silver of their cloak pins and shoe buckles.

Bebinn and Gerroc and I had hid one night beneath the table where the candlelight could not reach, listening to them talk about Athenry's banquets and horse races and the master builders working on the new stone wall and the abbey they were planning. Bebinn finally giggled and got us caught, of course.

But the truth was this: We'd had less meat than we needed when each set of visitors arrived, and *much* less when they'd left.

"Two lambs born today," Fallon said one evening over our scant supper of boiled barley.

"It's time," my mother said in her quiet way. I sighed, relieved. Lambs meant the ewes would be milked soon.

Fallon, as she did every year, left off her other work and went to help her uncle Cathal, the weaver, who kept more sheep than most. Each evening, she brought home a half pail of ewe's milk. Mother and I drank our portions gratefully, and I tried to be nice to Fallon in return. She was still glaring at me, so it was hard.

We all spun wool when we were otherwise idle. My mother was a fine spinner and had been a good weaver when she was younger, though she rarely used her straps and her loom now. Her hands ached from too many years of it. She wanted to teach me.

I wanted to be outside with the horses if I had time without work already filling it.

But I spun.

And spun.

There is no task so mindless, so peaceful, so *boring*.

By the twentieth day after Fallon had found her cracked comb, I began to worry less.

"Look at this," she said one evening, carrying in a full pail of ewe's milk. She set it on the little table near the fire. I thought she meant the milk, and I was about to exclaim over the joy of having a full pail instead of half when she extended her left hand, palm up, toward my mother. "Cellaig traded for my cracked one. He says he can use the carved part over again."

It was a new comb. She glanced at me. I looked straight at her, not blinking, keeping my face blank.

"That's good," my mother said. She glanced between us, feeling the tension. I hadn't told her about the comb—I hated it when she tried to protect me from Fallon and ended up with my father angry at her. He usually took Fallon's side against me.

"I am glad," I said evenly as I could. I meant it, for a number of reasons, as you may imagine.

"I have to work for him three days," Fallon added. She glanced at me again. "After lambing. I'll be cleaning raw bones he's had buried in dark soil all through the cold rains."

My mother wrinkled her nose, but Fallon didn't see her and I was grateful. I had done the same work once, trading for a brat clasp to fasten my brat tighter around my shoulders. It was terrible work, but old Cellaig was a kind-natured man and very skilled. His bone-and-antler carving was respected in other tuatha, not just our own. "I could help, perhaps," I said, wanting to make amends in my own way.

Fallon looked surprised. "If you can be spared elsewhere," she said, "I am sure the old man would welcome us both."

"I need her close just now," my mother said, saving me. Fallon nodded and sat down to her supper.

Early the next morning, my mother and I walked into the woods to gather dyestuffs. Bebinn and Gerroc saw us leave and only waved. They knew I loved to walk alone with my mother. She is a quiet woman and I often ended up talking for two, but she is good company and sometimes tells stories.

When her hands had begun aching too much to weave, she had learned dye craft from Orlaith. She was now outdoing the old woman. Since men are never allowed to attend dyeing, Mother colors cloth when my father is not here. This means she and I can stay up half the night tending the little fires beneath the dye pots, talking and laughing, without worry that he, or any other man, will come near and ruin the cloth.

In the woods that day, Mother made me lead the way, testing what I had learned. We gathered bracken for its yellowish green, lady's bedstraw for the gray it imparted to linen, and the lichen that grows on the oaks for the lovely red brown it gives when boiled with the cloth. We plant and grow our madder and our woad for red and blue—colors we are not allowed to wear.

The color laws are very strict. Free farmers can wear only dun brown, black, or yellow. Norman nobles—the lords to whom my father has to pay tributes and renders—wear red, gray, or dark brown. Above them, there were kings and queens who wore blue and purple, my mother said, a color that comes from some sea creature. Nothing has ever seemed sillier to me. Is a blue flower more noble than a yellow one?

That afternoon I helped her pulp woad from the garden. It is simple to pulp woad properly. You pound it until your arm breaks. Bebinn and Gerroc came to help, and we fell asleep in a heap by the fire, tired both from work and from being silly. My mother covered us with woolen blankets to keep us warm, and we did not wake until noon the next day. Our mothers milked for us that morning.

I had to wait until evening to see the gray mare, after the boys brought the mares back from grazing. I swung up onto her back and sat quietly for a long time as the stars came out. I imagined, as I often did, that I was riding, racing the wind through the meadows.

I told her that I wanted to keep her foal for my own, and she turned to nuzzle my bare leg. I slid off and put my arms around her neck. Perhaps she wanted me to have her foal? She might have. I knew she trusted me.

We dyed cloth again the next night. Gerroc could not come, but Bebinn and I stirred the pots and talked the night away. My father is proud of having traded one heifer and blue linen cloth to an armorer in Athenry for the sword he carries into battle against our enemies. My mother's dye pots saved him needing two cows to trade.

My father says the armorer in Athenry town is an Irish mastercrafter, but Athenry's fine stone wall and its tall keep belong to a Norman lord. I have never seen it, of course. I must rely on the tales my father tells.

My father says that Lord Birmingham, the Baron of Athenry, walks with his head high. He pretends not to see the beggars when winter is starving them. The people do not love him, my father says, not beggars nor crafters nor tuatha of farmers, ocaire or bonaire, free or bonded. It is not because he is a worse lord or a better one than any other. It is because he is not Irish, he is Norman. I wonder if Lord Birmingham of Athenry knows his townsman makes swords for his enemies.

CHAPTER THREE

🦋 🦋 🦋

The grass is growing now, and I cannot get enough of it.
The soft-voiced girl brings me handfuls of sweet grass every
morning before it is light. I feel heavy and slow.
How much longer before the foal comes?

I visited the gray mare every morning and
went back in the evening if I could. I could
see her flanks swelling. It would not be too much
longer before she foaled. Every time I opened the
rath gates, she whinnied when she saw me. It
lifted my heart to think I was a friend of such a
beautiful, kind creature.

I thought about showing Bebinn and Gerroc
the brooch, but instead I kept it to myself. I
wore it pinned on the underside of my brat near
my shoulder every day. It wasn't their hands I

mistrusted, or their hearts; it was their mouths. It was impossible to keep a secret in the tuath. Gerroc would tell her mother and Bebinn would confide in her favorite aunt. And then everyone would know. It was always that way. And Fallon would think that I *owed* her the brooch.

I know this sounds silly, but there you have it. Fallon's logic serves her well. She would say the faeries meant it for her, as a way for me to repay her for her broken comb.

As the days passed, while others were spinning and weaving and carving antlers and dyeing cloth and other tasks that needed finishing before Beltaine's feast brought other work for us to do, I was to begin spreading manure.

Lovely it was.

Lovely.

Lovely.

I wasn't alone, of course. Bebinn, Gerroc, and I were working together. And as we always did, we worked hard, but we also laughed and talked. We truly are sisters in our hearts.

Everyone in the tuath is related by blood, of course. Bebinn's father is my father's cousin, and so Fallon is her second cousin. I assure you she cannot stand Fallon's temper any more than I can. Bebinn's mother is connected to my father by marriage and by blood. Amlaíb, Gerroc's father, is my third cousin, though he is fifteen years older than I am.

Our bloodlines are as tangled as madder roots, my mother says, and I think she is right. I know that Bebinn, Gerroc, and I are bound by both blood and by love.

Manuring is a messy, smelly chore, as you may well imagine. We start piling it up after Samhain on November 1, when the cold weather starts. From Samhain to Imbolc, during the cold days of Gam, the stock is shut into the earthen-walled rath much of the time. The piles get bigger as the days pass. Manure, piled like that, rots so fast that it steams and gives off heat like fire embers. On the coldest nights, I have seen the mares standing close to the piles for warmth.

By the time we are past Imbolc, coming into early spring, the men haul it to the fields to richen the soil for our seeds.

If they are home, of course.

This year, they weren't.

Day after warm sunny day, the men did not come home. So it was up to us. Most years, the men used an ox or a horse to pull the manure drags. This year, the oxen were thinner than usual and weak with scours. My mother and some of the others had decided to give them betony as a cure, but it wasn't working yet. Because the men were off at war, their horses were all gone as well. We were left with the broodmares and they were all in foal. No one wanted to work a mare hard enough to risk losing her foal.

We had little choice. Heavy work or no, it had to be done. Who better to do it than girls who were not expert at anything else yet?

For this chore, along with helping with pig slaughter and anything else that ruined clothes, we always wore our last year's leinte. Bebinn had shot up like willow in the rain, and so she was bare halfway to her knees.

We used drags made from stiff leather. We tied plaited ropes at the corners of the stiff cowhides, piled as much of the dark, rotted manure on top as we could, then pulled them along over the grassy ground, all the way down to the barley fields. Manure is astoundingly heavy. We staggered forward against the weight, digging our bare toes into the soft dirt.

It was a good long way and we had to stop several times to catch our breath. Once there, we lurched forward, stopping every ten steps, using oaken pitchforks to scatter the manure over the soil until we had unloaded it all.

Back and forth.

The pig-herd boys called out, teasing Bebinn about her bare legs when they passed us as they drove the sows from one end of our woods to the other. Bebinn ignored them, all but Tally. At him, she made a face. It's no secret they are drawn together. I am sure they will marry. Gerroc and I have no such luck, at least not yet. All the boys look the same to us.

The best part about manuring was getting to see the gray mare so many times in one day. Every time we came back to load our drag, she whinnied at me and I took a moment to stand beside her.

"That horse loves you," Bebinn said when we stopped to rest halfway to the fields.

I looked at her. "I am going to ask my father for her foal."

Bebinn and Gerroc both opened their mouths, then closed them. I knew why. Horses are for men and boys, everyone knows. My father certainly thought so. I had to change his mind.

"Are you working or talking?" Fallon shouted, walking along a path that led to the creek. No one answered her, but we all picked up the drag and began to pull.

The manuring took us a full ten days, dark to dark. It didn't help that we were hungry. We ate very little at noon and less at evening meal. When we finally finished, we went back to our usual chores, but now we took turns milking.

There were only four cows giving anything at all. When it was not my turn, I spent the morning time visiting with the gray mare. She whickered when she saw me coming, and it made my spirit light and happy to hear her voice.

I swung up onto her back and lay flat, pressed against her warmth. She always stood quietly, reaching around to touch my foot with her muzzle.

CHAPTER FOUR

ლ ლ ლ

*The girl stands close and leans against me. There was
another girl once, not so kind as this one. This one knows
when to be quiet, and her hair smells like the woods. I am
always glad to hear her footsteps.*

I loved having time to myself when either
Bebinn or Gerroc was milking. It lasted only
until my mother noticed me idling, of course.
That morning, we dug a pit for a cauldron fire.
We boiled tallow for candles—another terrible,
smelly job, but thankfully it lasted only a few days.

I was grateful when lambing slowed and Fallon
decided to help her cousins break flax. It had
been buried beneath the dark surface of the wet
soil in a boggy corroc, then had been twenty days
soaking in the creek, weighed down by stones.

Now the stems were rotten and ready to peel. The fibers inside the thick flax stems spin the same as wool, but are lighter and stronger.

Since the creek was on the far side of our tuath's land, Fallon decided to sleep there rather than walk home weary each night.

That evening my mother told me Fallon would be gone from us for ten additional, glorious days or more. I tried hard not to smile. She tried hard not to notice me trying hard. My mother is unfailingly kind, but I knew that Fallon's presence in our house was hard for her much of the time.

That evening, and those that followed, were peaceful. With my father off to war and Fallon breaking flax, it was just the two of us making our barley suppers, sometimes eating a bit of old, hard cheese my mother had tucked away and saved for a time like this one. I loved sitting with her on the wide oaken bench that stands in our yard just past the herb garden, talking in the dark.

"You have become a fine cheesemaker," my mother said to me one evening. I felt my cheeks go pink. She loves me with all her heart, I know that, but she is not one for praise. So when it comes, I blush. "I am getting better, I know," I said modestly.

"I am sure this year you will make cheese as good as any of the grown women of the tuath," she said.

I managed a long breath. "Thank you for saying so, Mother," I answered.

She looked at me. I could see the shine of her white skin in the moonlight. "You do all your work well. Last year, when you helped me birth calves and foals, you had as steady a hand as any."

I smiled. "I love the horses, Mother."

She nodded. "I know you do. It is a pity you are not a boy."

I sat up straighter, looking into her eyes. "I love foals' breath, sweet with milk. I love their hooves, small enough to fit in my cupped hand. I don't love weaving or embroidery or dyeing."

Mother nodded, but she refused to discuss the impossible again. She had told me a dozen times. Horses were for men, for war, for hunting and plowing and riding off to deliver tribute and visit lords.

The only reason my mother helped mares and cows having trouble birthing was that the men wanted nothing to do with it. I had helped her a dozen times when a foal or calf was in the wrong position and needed turning or straightening to come into the world. It was like a miracle, every time. I loved to smell the odd salt-sweet scent of mare's breath when they were close to birthing. My mother said she could not smell it, but I could. And I loved to see the foals take their first breath.

"I want to teach you the rest of the dye plants this year before you and the girls go to the high pastures," she said.

I knew my mother wanted me to learn all I could. But her mentioning the high pastures made my stomach tighten. Bebinn and Gerroc and I were all excited and a little nervous about going for the first time that year. I was hoping that my mother could come with us, if my father would allow her.

"You will be grown and gone before I can believe it has happened," she said. She went silent then, and I waited. My mother can take a good long time to speak her mind, but when she does, she says precisely what she means. I am like my father. I open my lips, and words tumble out, wrong or right.

"I have been meaning to ask if there is a boy you fancy," my mother said slowly.

I shook my head so hard my hair slapped my cheeks. "No. Not a one."

She laughed. "I was like you are, Lara. There is no need to hurry it, to my mind anyway. It'll come quick enough. I'll tell your father and do my best but . . . "

Her voice faded and stopped, and I knew what she was thinking. Fallon had not wanted to choose a boy and look what had happened to her. None had ever chosen her. She was nearly fifteen now, so cross and angry that none of the boys her own age wanted a thing to do with her. The older men and the widowers stepped around her even more warily. If she was not promised by now, there was a chance she never would be.

Bebinn's eldest sister was an old woman of thirty now and she had never been married a day. She lived with one of Bebinn's brothers and his wife. If a woman didn't marry, she never had her own house, never her own life.

"I just don't want to be shoved along," I said quietly.

My mother took in a long breath. "I will do what I can to keep your father out of it."

"Thank you, Mother," I said, and I meant it. Standing up to my father was no task for a coward, and he would want me married sooner than later.

"He should be home soon," my mother said quietly.

"Did he say when?" I asked, knowing my father rarely told her anymore. He was tired of breaking his own promises.

My mother was nodding. "He did. He said he would try to be back before summer's start, before Beltaine."

"Try?" I asked. "Try or would?"

My mother frowned deeper. "Try. But I think he will. He knows that we will need all the men here by then, to plow and plant. Though I am glad your brothers are not here," she added, without saying anything more.

I knew what she meant. Fergal and Trian were

farther west a good deal, close to the sea and away from Athenry's Norman lords. Unless things got worse, they would be clear of most of the fighting. It all seemed so senseless to me. The Irish clans fought one another, they all fought the Normans, and no one ever managed to have a year without sorrows in the tuath, men who lost their lives in the fighting—or women starving at home waiting for men who never returned.

"So it should be very soon," my mother said.

I smiled vacantly, not wishing to remind her that he had said the same thing the year before, then had not come home until nearly a fortnight after summer had begun. I wondered if we women and girls would be plowing again this year.

CHAPTER FIVE

✺ ✺ ✺

Another mare had her foal this morning. It is a slender babe, nearly black, with big, curious eyes. The girl came in time to see the foal slide into the world. She stayed close, singing a gentle song, calm and quiet and watchful. Not one of us minded her being here.

*O*n the ninth morning without Fallon, I came back from the mares to the sound of my mother weeping. I leaped up the path and ran past the garden, startled and scared. She was standing in the dooryard, the sun barely up, chickens pecking at her bare toes. They were as hungry as the rest of us.

"What?" I asked her, breathless. "What is it?"

"Your father," she said in a low voice. "Something has happened to him. In battle." She heaved a breath in, then out again. "Fighting.

With O'Flaherty's men against de Burgo's."

My mother can sometimes know something she can't possibly know. It scares me when it happens. "Are you sure?" I asked her, keeping my voice even as I could. "Maybe it was just a sleep fancy?" She shook her head. "Do we have a guest? Did someone tell you this?" She didn't answer.

I put my hands on her shoulders and turned her to face me, to make sure of what she was saying. She shrugged off my hands and then took them in her own. "No. No one has been here. But it is as true as the mist, Lara." She waved one hand to indicate the dripping fog that lay over the earth, hiding the edge of the forest on the far side of our unplanted barley fields.

I nodded, pulling in a long, barbed breath of my own. My mother's sudden *knowings* came seldom and were usually true. Her mother, my grandmother, had been the same way, always knowing things before she had any way *to* know them.

I hoped fiercely that I had not inherited my mother's gift as a seer. I did not want the sadness that came with it—or the trouble. Any woman among us who had the sight kept it close and quiet.

The priests and churchmen who came sometimes to guest with us did not like to hear about any of the old ways. It was fair, I suppose. There were a good number among us who were still wary of what my mother called the new ways.

"Ach, Lara," my mother said, wiping at her eyes. "We must think what to do. If he lives, he will be here soon and we have no food and we cannot hunt until Samhain Feast in November and until the cows come back into milk we just don't have . . . " She trailed off, her voice shaky.

It unnerved me. My mother is almost never anything but calm. I hugged her close a moment. I was a little taller than she was now and it felt strange. I was soon going to be much taller than she ever would be. This was strange, too: She was slack in my arms, exhausted. It was as though, for that instant, I was the mother and she was the weary child.

She stepped back after a moment and walked forward, stiff-kneed, floor straw sill clinging to her bare feet. I shooed the chickens into the grass, then turned to see my mother sitting on the smooth oaken bench my father had made for her before I was born.

She turned slightly, angled away from me. I knew she wanted to be alone, but I couldn't make myself leave her. I was scared. What would become of us if my father never came home? I am ashamed to say I knew that I would not miss him—he had never been very kind to me— and it seemed to me that he was rarely with us anyway. He was often gone from Samhain to Imbolc, fighting and hunting, living in the forests with his men. Or, like this year, he might be gone all the way on to Beltaine and the start of summer.

But if my father ceased to live and was no longer rí of our tuath, who would step forward to rule us and make judgments on people's arguments? Who would deal with the Norman Baron of Athenry and all his demands for cattle and corn and whatever else he thought we had? One of my brothers? Neither Fergal nor Trian was near old enough yet.

I found myself staring at the bench. I usually leaped over it as I came and went, pretending to be a wild horse, galloping off to freedom. Some mornings pretending to be a wild mare was far better than being myself, off to work, shivery and cold beneath a dripping gray sky.

The bench had been made from the massive trunk of an old, old oak. It had taken my father several long days to cut it, several more days to drag it home with the oxen, then many more days with adze and ax and sweat to shape it.

And he had done it for my mother.

In his own harsh, angry way, he loved her. And me. No matter what jumble feelings I had toward him, the whole tuath depended on him. And my mother loved him desperately.

I sat there, saying silent prayers, then begging faeries and the old gods and goddesses to bring my father home safe. I slid my hand beneath my brat and touched the horse brooch pinned there. The gold was always warm from my skin now.

I listened to the families of our tuath waking up. I heard boys' shouts, then the horses neighing back and forth as they were let out of the rath for their day's grazing. Then the smell of wood smoke crept through the mist and I knew people were just beginning to rekindle their fires.

My mother finally spoke. "Bebinn's mother asked for your help today," she said. "Clearing and manuring her house garden." I nodded. My mother looked small to me, hunched over on the oaken bench. Shivering and still uneasy, thinking about her *knowing*, I went in and blew on the white ashes that covered last night's embers, then placed brittle oak twigs on them. I waited until I saw the first curl of smoke, then I fanned it with a handful of my brat, flapping the cloth until the flames came up. I set two thick sticks across the kindling, then a small log. The flames crackled and the hot smoke rose to the roof hole.

I made my mother some steaming barley water in our little iron pot. Then I broke a bit of cheese from her tiny store. She was right. We had very little food left. If the cows didn't begin dropping their calves soon—and coming into milk again— there would be worse hunger.

"We shouldn't eat that," my mother said when she saw the cheese. "We should save whatever bits of food we have for your father when he comes."

Knowing she would say that, I had an answer

ready. She was right in one way, but in another way, she was wrong. "You will need strength to nurse him if he is hurt," I reminded her.

After a long moment, she nodded and took the food from me. I saw her breathing in the steam from the barley water before she sipped it. I watched her eat. The food calmed her as I had hoped it would. Her eyes lost the wild look. She was getting too thin—thinner than she usually got this time of year. Everyone was, though. It was a lean year, indeed.

"The bay mare had her foal," I said.

My mother smiled, her face still dreamy and odd. "No trouble?"

I shook my head. "No. The baby came out perfectly, his little front hooves, then his muzzle, then the rest of him. He's a beauty."

She nodded. "I have wished for this sometimes."

I didn't know what she meant, so I just waited for her to go on.

"I have wished that he would get hurt—just hurt enough to learn that all this warring is madness, that we need him here."

I took a breath, thinking that my father seemed miserable when he was here, that he loved his warring and adventuring more than he loved either of us, but I didn't say it. I knew my father only partly, as any daughter knows her father. It was my mother who had seen his whole heart.

I looked up to see Bebinn and Gerroc coming up the path, ready to begin the day's work. I made a quick little motion like I was shooing sheep. They hesitated, then veered off, understanding that we had a need to be alone, my mother and I.

When my mother rose to go inside, I followed and sat with her until she had fallen back to sleep by the fire. Then I tiptoed out, hoping she would sleep until afternoon.

I ran up the valley path so I could come close to where the mares were grazing. The little black foal was unsteady on his long legs and adorable, tottering beside his mother as she grazed.

The herd boys saw me and a few of them called out, teasing me, calling me an odd-looking horse boy, asking if I was lost.

"Be still," Tally finally shouted. "You sound like hens. Did one of you lay an egg?"

That made them all laugh and blush at the same time. I shot him a grateful glance and he nodded at me, a tiny motion that no one else would notice. For a moment I envied Bebinn. Tally was kind.

While the boys were preoccupied with wondering why Tally had stood up for me, I made my way into the herd, talking quietly to the mares. Most of them didn't so much as look up, but the gray mare lifted her head and walked toward me, extending her muzzle. I touched her cheek, then laid my hand on her forehead, trying not to cry while I whispered what had happened. There was no one else I could tell. It would upset everyone in the tuath to think my father had been hurt.

When I knew I could smile, I turned and left, walking until I was clear of the mares, then breaking into a run. I thought about riding. I wanted a horse of my own, a horse I could ride fast as wind and loud as thunder through the meadows. Not riding to wars like the men, not to battles, but for the sheer joy of it.

"What happened?" Bebinn asked me when I got to her cottage. I glanced at her, then at the sky, then back at her. I was reluctant to tell the truth, but I didn't want to lie.

"Don't tell me if you don't want to," she said. I knew she meant it, but I could also tell that she was hurt. I felt the brooch beneath my brat, the metal smooth and warm. If I kept this secret, it would mean I had *two*.

Gerroc made a sound of impatience. "Tell us. If it is a bad thing, we can help. If it is simply shameful, we won't tell. If it is—"

"My mother is worried about my father," I interrupted her, telling half the truth. "She barely sleeps."

They both nodded. Their fathers were with mine, of course, wherever he was.

"I have been thinking about it," I said quietly.

Bebinn shook her head. "Maybe it's just like the seasons or the tides or the forests. Maybe it can't be changed."

No one knew what else to say, so we didn't try. We fell to work and had the dried stalks and matted roots out of their garden bed before noon. Then we made one last trip to the rath for manure and dragged it back, talking again. I told them about the foal and how Tally had been kind to me.

I kept glancing at the edge of the forest, imagining that I heard hoofbeats, listening for someone's dogs to bark. But my father did not come home that evening.

What a strange day. Things were either good or awful.

The awful: My mother had a terrible vision.

Fallon came home that evening.

The good: A beautiful foal was born, and we finished the very, very, *very* last of this year's manuring.

CHAPTER SIX

❦ ❦ ❦

My foal is growing inside me. It moves now, as though it is dreaming of galloping across endless fields.

allon barely spoke from weariness her first night back with us. She rose early and told me that after the backbreaking toil over the flax pits, she was going to gather herbs in the woods for a day or two. She left without saying any more than that.

My mother stayed on her pallet by the fire pit while I got up and readied myself for the day's work. It was so unlike her that I found myself thinking that I should not leave her.

"I am not ill," she promised me.

"Are you sure?" I asked her.

She nodded. "Go on about your work, Lara."

I started toward the door, then turned back.

She rolled herself over to face me. "I am just wishing your father would come home today so that I can tend to him. I worry about him every day that he is gone, visions or no. Knowing he is hurt, I worry more."

I nodded. Her *knowing* made me nervous enough to want to leave without talking anymore, but I planted my feet and faced her. "Mother," I began, keeping my voice level. "I will check the broodmares, then I will milk—it's my turn today. Then I will come back."

She smiled. I waited for her to say something, and when she didn't, I tried to smile back at her. "If I hear Father coming home," I told her, "I will run back from the dairy and help you in any way you need."

"I thank you for that, Lara," she said. "You are a good daughter."

She was smiling, but her eyes looked hollowed and I knew that she hadn't been sleeping—just lying still in the darkness, worrying all night.

I took a long breath. "You might be wrong. Father might not be hurt."

She waved my words away with a gesture. "Fallon should be told—she is his sister after all."

I set down my milk pail—the cows would not mind if I was late this time of year when they had so little milk. "I don't want to tell Fallon only to be wrong, Mother. You know how angry she gets. She would never forgive either one of us for giving her a meaningless worry." I cleared my throat. "She still holds anger against me for something I did not do."

My mother tilted her head, but asked no questions, and I was grateful not to have to tell her about Magnus and the comb. "Go now," she said after a long silence.

I met her eyes. "Are you sure?"

She smiled again. "I am awake now and there is much to do. I am going to clean today, rake the floor straw out and find fresh. I want to cut rushes for a new pallet."

I went back to her and squatted on my heels to kiss her cheek. Then I went out the door, still thinking I should stay, but knowing in my heart that I didn't want to. It made me uneasy to be around my mother when she was so certain of something that scared me. I wanted to argue with her. I wanted her to be wrong.

I walked fast in the cold morning air and followed the long curve of the rath's earthen wall around to the opening. I set my milk pail beneath the oak tree, then pushed open the heavy wooden gates. The mares in the rath looked up when the planks creaked.

They whickered and gathered around me, some of them smelling my leine, then my hair. The gray mare came close, then she stayed at my side as I walked through the herd to make sure there were no new babies. There weren't. I was happy anyway.

I loved how they all trusted me. And more than all of them put together, I loved the gray mare.

I stood with the mare as long as I dared, rubbing her ears and leaning against her side to keep warm. I pressed my hands against her flanks. I could feel her foal stretching and moving beneath her skin.

"I want to be close when you give birth," I told

her. She turned her head, reaching back to nibble at my ear. "I'll be quiet and careful," I promised. "And I'll get my mother if you need any real help."

The mare whickered softly and switched her tail. I felt the foal inside her move again, the biggest bulge was now farther back on her side. That meant the birthing was getting closer.

"When there is a foal," I whispered, "I will help dry it and help it stand up if you will let me."

I smiled in the dim light that comes before dawn and turned to rub another mare's jaw. "I will love all your babies," I promised as they milled around me.

I looked up at the sky. It was softening from black to gray. Soon the mares would be let out to graze. How I envied the boys who would get to watch them all day.

I forced myself to head back toward the gates and tried not to think about my mother, cleaning the floors and airing the house for my father—my *wounded* father, as she believed. There was enough to suffer this time of year without more, and so much work to do as the weather warmed as we got closer to Beltaine and the proper beginning of summer. It was time to plow and to plant, and most of our men were with my father, which meant the women and the boys would have to make do as best we could. And we were all hungrier than usual this year.

Leaving, I slid the bar back across the gate to lock it closed and fetched my milk pail. Crossing the fields, I heard Bebinn's giggle and Gerroc saying something low.

There were dogs barking in the distance and I listened for a moment, my heart speeding up. But the dogs quieted. It was not my father and the men. It wasn't anything.

"There you are," Bebinn called. "I hoped to find you before you milked."

Gerroc was with her. We were all used to rising before the sun. "It's my turn today," I reminded them.

Bebinn held out a leathern cup. "My mother asked me to beg a little milk for her barley water. We'll help with the milking."

I nodded, but I wanted every drop of milk I could get to take back to my mother. Some had their own cows, but most families shared, and the households were supposed to take turns now.

"This one has almost nothing left to give us," Bebinn said sadly as she led her first cow into the milking stall and tied her halter to the post.

"None of them do," Gerroc agreed. "We should just let them dry up to be ready for their calves when they come."

We all nodded, but no one had told us to stop milking yet, even though the celebration of Beltaine was not far off, and the gamuin, the few winter calves that were allowed this year, were long since weaned.

The feast of Beltaine would be pork and little else this year, I was sure. Every house had gone through its stores. No one had cattle to spare—we all had very little cheese left. The peas, celeriac, and leeks of last summer were long since eaten. Usually, by this time, the apples were nearly gone, too.

"I am so hungry," Gerroc said quietly as I milked.

When I was done, I stood up with barely half a pail. It was less than I had hoped for, but more than I had feared. I gave Bebinn half a cup.

"It can't last much longer," Gerroc said wistfully.

Bebinn and I nodded agreement.

"I am dreaming of summer plums," Gerroc whispered.

Bebinn and I glanced at each other.

"Apples," Bebinn said. "Hot, roasted apples. And pea soup with new bread."

My mouth filled with saliva and my stomach cramped. "Shh," I said, irritated. "What good is talk like that?"

Gerroc lowered her eyes and I was instantly sorry. "I am just so hungry," I said apologetically.

Bebinn nodded. "I don't remember another year this bad."

"I have to go," I said. "My mother needs something to eat and I don't want to leave her alone too long."

And it was at that instant that we heard the shouts and the hoofbeats.

CHAPTER SEVEN

ℜ ℜ ℜ

*It all happened so fast. I had no time to try to break away
from the other mares. The men panicked us all with their
shouting and the leather whips cracking over our heads
and stinging our backs.*

All three of us ran outside. The sky was
paling to gray blue, the eastern horizon
turning gold. We could just see the edge of the
forest and the horsemen riding toward us.

For an instant I thought it was my father and
his men, and I was joyous because the man lead-
ing the others up the hill rode tall and straight.
Then I realized that though he might be someone's father, he was not mine.

"Run!" I shouted. "Run home!"

I hitched my leine up above my knees and

sprinted for my house, glancing back to see Bebinn and Gerroc flying over the ground in the opposite direction, their bare legs flashing.

I veered to pass behind the old rath, hiding myself as the men galloped closer. My chest began to ache, but I did not stop. I managed to reach our door and found my mother frantic and frightened—for me.

"Hide yourself," she called.

I shook my head, too winded to speak, but she didn't see me. She was already running for the rath, convinced, I suppose, that she might manage to save a horse or two from the raiders.

I could hear shouts as the battle began. It would be short and easy for the raiders—like pushing children out of the way. There wasn't anyone to defend us, really, only old men and little boys. I heard barking, but knew that my father and the other men had taken the hunting hounds with them as well. Even our dogs were puppies or lame with age.

Shouting at my mother, I followed her back toward the rath and finally caught up, dragging her with me to hide beneath the low oak branches as the raiders thundered toward us. Whether they saw us or not, I will never know. I suppose they didn't care; they were after the horses.

We crouched there, our arms locked together, both of us trembling as the strangers opened the gates and rode inside, herding the mares at a gallop back in the direction they had come from.

Others were riding hard behind our four dry dairy cows and they pounded past us, all of them whooping and cheering as they rode back to wherever they had come from. The sun was rising. They rode straight toward it.

Were they from the east, somewhere, then? I longed for my father to come home. To *be* home. He would ride after these men and get the gray mare back.

When the sun rose and shone on our faces, it found us pale and frightened. My mother shook herself once the raiders were long gone and obviously not coming back. She looked at me. "Come, we have work to do. Hold your head up."

We walked from house to house. Most were all right. One old man had been hurt. We found him in the woods, waiting for help to come.

Magnus was missing, too, for a few hours, but then we found him. He had crawled into a woodpile and the logs had shifted and trapped him. He was scared, but safe. I cried and hugged him close when they got him out.

We found the bay mare at the edge of the woods. Her foal was limping with her, but not too badly. Somehow, she had managed to drop back between the riders' whips when her foal could not keep up. We brought her back up the hill and put her and her foal inside the rath.

But Bebinn, my sweet almost-sister Bebinn, was gone. Just *gone*.

No one had seen her captured. No one knew if she had been hurt and lay in the woods somewhere or if she had been carried off.

I could not stop crying for her, praying to all the old gods and all the saints that she was not badly hurt, not dead. And that if she had been captured, she would get away and come back to us.

Bebinn's mother was calm because her other children needed her to be calm. I could see the agony in her eyes, though.

We all walked through the woods, close enough

together to touch hands, calling, looking beneath budding plum thickets. By evening, my mother called a halt to the searching.

Gerroc and I cried together where no one could see us—so our sorrow would not hurt Bebinn's family more than they already hurt.

While there was still light, we all kept going from one house to the next, even though there was nothing new to tell. We just walked one way, then back, Gerroc and I holding hands in our misery, following our mothers. She was limping a little. She had twisted her ankle running.

Little Magnus's and Gerroc's older brothers had tried to fight and had been hurt, but not badly. Their cuts and bruises were no worse than they sometimes gave one another. They were all very proud that they had tried to protect our tuath. I could hear their tales of battle growing with each telling.

Later, when I could think past Bebinn's disappearance for a moment, I mourned the loss of the mares. I prayed to the saints and old gods that they would be treated well, their foals treated kindly, raised to trust. And the gray mare, with her gentle spirit and patience, was the subject of many of my pleadings. She had loved me, I thought. I knew I had loved her. I had been so excited to see her foal.

That terrible day passed in a blur of tears.

I wept for Bebinn, for myself, missing her laughter, her smiles, and the way she wrinkled her nose when she was annoyed. Everything about her was clear to me, now that she was gone. Gerroc and I sat close together after the search, understanding each other's misery perfectly, and later, off by myself, I wept for the gray mare.

That evening, my mother shook me by my shoulders and told me to stop weeping. "We are lucky," she said, her voice sharp. "You had never seen a raid until today and you are rising ten. In the old days, you'd have seen twenty by now."

I nodded slowly. I knew it was true. All the old people told stories they had heard as children, and most of them were about raids and tuaths destroyed, then rebuilt. And about bigger wars.

My mother reached to push my hair out of my face. "Lara, we have much to be thankful for. The raiders did not find the big herd of cattle—the boys had them off in the lower fields to graze. They did not bother the boys chasing pigs in the woods or steal our chickens or kill our dogs. They did not burn our houses." She put her hands on her hips. "We will not starve. And captives are rarely killed now—it's not like the tales the men tell of the old times. Your father is a warrior other men fear. For that reason she will likely not be harmed, just held. Be thankful for that."

I nodded and squared my shoulders. She handed me a basket of calming herbs to take to Bebbin's mother.

I tried to walk tall, to keep from crying. I passed Fallon at the bottom of our hill and she barely nodded at me, striding off on some errand of her own. She was in a fury over the raid, talking to everyone about how my father would make the thieves pay dearly. She had spent a long time pacing in circles, shaking her fist in the direction the riders had gone. I had left her alone. Everyone did.

"Will they come back?" I asked my mother that first night, once everyone except Gerroc had gone home, to make what small meals they could from their scanty stores.

She shook her head. "They had a long way to ride—only fools rob close neighbors."

Gerroc took a breath. "I looked into their faces as carefully as I could; I knew none of them."

My mother was nodding. "None looked like anyone I know."

I blinked. Gerroc was right. The O'Cloughs were tall and thin; most had ice blue eyes. We were shorter and heavier, almost all of us with straight brown hair—Bebinn's red tangle was a rarity among us. If these raiders had come from any family we knew, we would have recognized them.

Even though my mother reassured everyone and sent boys to three nearby tuatha to raise the watch for raiders, I don't think anyone slept that night. I know I did not.

I woke next morning in the dark and lay still, my eyes filling with tears over Bebinn. What work could I do without my dear friend? How could I live without ever again hearing her laughter?

"Do not assume the worst," my mother said softly in the darkness. Had she been awake all night? "Bebinn might manage to come back to us," she added. "If not, she might marry in the new place . . ." She trailed off, and I knew she was thinking exactly what I was thinking.

Tally.

I felt terrible. I had been so lost in my own hurt and worry that I hadn't once given his a thought. I forced myself to rise and washed my face in the yard basin. I touched the little brooch pinned on the underside of my brat. What princess of the old times had worn it? How many cattle raids had she survived? The warring had been even worse long ago, my mother had said.

That first terrible morning after the raid, I went inside the rath and talked to the bay mare. Her foal was standing steadier, and I was glad. But my heart was heavy.

No one sang that morning, or whistled. Our whole tuath was silent. Gerroc and I walked side by side in the dawn dark on our way to milk. We held hands; it would have been Bebinn's turn that day.

CHAPTER EIGHT

🎠 🎠 🎠

These men are driving us hard, too hard. My legs ache,
and the foal inside me is frightened because I am. Where
are they taking us? Don't they know we need rest and a
quiet place when we are so close to foaling?

*F*our nights later, I was sitting beside our
dying cookfire, wishing the sun would hurry
and go down so I could lose my sorrows in
sleep. When I heard hoofbeats, I went rigid for
an instant, glancing at my mother. We crept
outside, ready to run. But this time there was no
need. This time, it *was* my father, galloping his
big bay gelding up the hill. He was sitting straight
and shouting, and I rejoiced, thinking that my
mother's famous *knowing* had been wrong for
once.

His men rode with him, all of them shouting and whooping as they came up the hill. The hounds ran silent, their tongues hanging out. The men dropped back a little as they got closer, letting my father lead the way, then all reined in, pulling their sweating horses to a halt in front of our house.

My father dismounted slowly, and only then did I realize he was using one arm. My mother had been right, as always, but my heart was still unburdened to see him smiling, looking strong in spite of the bloody wound across his left forearm. I saw a crease in his shield and wondered what mighty blow had done it. The one that had wounded him?

I shivered and looked back at my mother. I could see in her eyes that she was overwhelmed with happiness to see him alive and acting like himself. I knew, too, that she was glad to have him home where she could tend to him.

I was not so sure about what I felt, as always. When my father was home, everything changed. I stood back a little, watching. The men laughed as my tall, broad father swung my little, bird-boned mother around in a circle with his one good arm around her waist and her arms around his neck. They shouted jests and spun their horses around, acting like boys.

It was always like this when my father came home.

At first, anyway.

The hounds barked, then slunk off in the dark to find water and their familiar sleep dens behind the houses. The men quieted when they saw the look on my mother's face when my father set her down and she stepped back. "Please listen," she said quietly.

They were silent as she described the raid, told them that all the mares but one had been taken—and Bebinn. She told the story of how we had found Magnus and told them all the old man was doing all right. She left nothing out and no one interrupted her.

"I'm off to see to my own wife, then," a voice came out of the near dark the moment my mother stopped speaking. I recognized it. Bebinn's father.

"Take my horse," my father said, passing the

reins to Magnus's eldest brother. "Close them all in the rath and carry your saddle pads and bridles home. Sleep with your ears open," he added, then turned to embrace my mother with one arm again.

The men cantered off, and I heard their voices in the dark as they settled their tired horses for the night. I heard them calling farewells to one another as they headed toward their homes and families. Moments later, I heard laughter and children's shouts spread from one house to the next. The glow of rekindled fires lightened the open doorways.

"Lara?"

"Yes, Father?" I answered respectfully, jolted out of my dreamy eavesdropping.

"Come in out of the damp."

"Yes, Father," I answered him, and turned for the door.

He had built up the fire, and my mother had wrapped his forearm in a piece of clean linen. It had been torn from a length of her finest soft cloth, dyed the beautiful blue only royalty were allowed to wear. My father looked content. My mother was boiling a handful of barley. It smelled wonderful and my mouth watered.

"I hope you girls are nearly ready to take the cattle to the upland pastures," my father said, looking at me. "We will need the milk and cheese sorely this year, your mother tells me." His chin lifted and he narrowed his eyes. "You've grown."

I nodded. "I am taller than Mother now."

"Only a little," she said, pretending offense to make him laugh.

He didn't notice. He nodded absently, already thinking past such a small thing as my height.

"The fields are manured," I said, and was rewarded with an approving nod. "We cleaned chicken byres and the rath," I added. I recited all the chores I could think of, watching his face brighten a little with each one. He looked at my mother and nodded. I knew that was all the thanks either of us would get for all the weary days of hard work since we had seen him last.

"In the morning," he said, "plowing can begin." He looked at my mother. "How many days until Beltaine?"

She glanced up, counting. "Eight."

He nodded. "The morning after Beltaine, we'll get the cows away and up onto the high pastures and good grass. Before that, we will plow and plant and gather wood and all else that we need to do. Once we are settled for summer, once the crops are in the ground, I'll ride after the raiders."

I swallowed hard. I understood. I did. I knew the men had to stay to plow and plant—we were all hungry and we had months to go before harvest. Delaying it could easily mean starvation for some of us. But I still wanted them to ride after Bebinn *now*, this very night.

I saw my father glance at my mother, and an uneasy look crossed his face. I looked at her, and realized he hadn't seen her for months. She had become so thin—and she looked very tired.

"Tell us a tale," she said, her eyes reflecting the firelight.

My father began to talk. He told us of a buck as tall as a horse that he had seen in the forest, of a storm that had blown an oak down, of the stone-walled castle in Athenry and the stone wall that had been built around the town.

Then, as the fire wore itself out and the embers glowed in the dark house, he spoke of battles he had fought. There was a new alliance with what was left of the O'Flaherty clan near Galway, wherever that was. They had driven the Normans back from old Tuam, he said.

My mother nodded and made sounds of interest, but I saw her staring out at the open door into the night. I wondered if her thoughts were the same as mine. What good was winning battles if Bebinn had been carried off? Would winning battles feed us? It never had. If he had stayed home to protect us, the planting would be done, we would still have our horses, and dear Bebinn would be in her own home this night.

I sat close to the dying fire and thought about going up to the high pasture with the others. This would be my first year to help. I had been scared and excited about it—before—when Bebinn and Gerroc and I were to have gone together. It would have been the first time for all three of us.

Now the idea of leaving our rath and the houses of our tuath scared me. What if raiders came to the upland pastures? What if all the stock was stolen? How would we live? I had heard about raids all of my life. *In stories.* Somehow I had never understood that the stories were real.

I lay down with my cold, dark thoughts and listened to my parents whispering long into the night. I could only hear part of what they said clearly enough to understand, and some of that made no sense to me anyway.

After asking him three times, each time in a different way, my mother finally got an answer about whether or not the battles had been won or lost.

"Both," my father said. He sounded weary now. I could imagine the sparkle going out of his eyes. "The Normans in Galway town are there to stay, I fear, and in Athenry. But the O'Flahertys will keep them worried and push the O'Connors back into their place, at least."

My mother was silent, and I knew she was hoping he would say more.

"Ireland has only once had her own king," my father said bitterly. "We've had Norse invaders from the sea and men from the saints only know where else, and these Normans, let in by

Strongbow, the fool, building their keeps and castles and abbeys. And the only one who united us all against them was Brian Boru."

My father turned and spat into the fire pit. The sudden hissing startled me and my heart leaped.

"His reign was all too short," my father said in a voice so low I could barely hear him. "And all too long ago." He pulled in a long breath. "And Irishmen raid each other's horses and cattle instead of fighting Normans."

His voice was heavy with fatigue and discouragement, and I wondered if they all sounded like him tonight, talking to their wives. I knew Gerroc would lie awake, listening, that Magnus would, too. And then I wondered where Bebinn was, and I had to turn over to hide my crying.

CHAPTER NINE

✿ ✿ ✿

We gallop to one place, then another, then back. It is like it was before. These men do not travel to reach another place. They travel to hide, or to attack. There are more horses now. I am tired; all the mares that are in foal are weary.

*T*he next morning, my father mounted his horse and rode at a gallop from one end of the tuath to the other, looking at the state of the fields, the cattle, the sheep, shouting out orders, setting tasks for everyone.

I was walking with Gerroc, on our way back from a milking so scant we had barely enough milk to fill a cup. My father was riding hard, shouting over his shoulder at Gerroc's oldest brother and her uncle. They both nodded and started off at a run.

"Your father is so brave," Gerroc said to me. "My father says he fights harder than any of them, takes all the risks on himself if he can."

I watched my father pivot his gelding, lifting him back into a gallop as he kept everyone working at a pace few liked, but all saw as necessary, now that he was here to organize things again.

"My father says he would follow yours to the stars and back," Gerroc said.

I watched as the big bay gelding galloped out of sight. My father was like the old kings, I realized, like the ones in the stories. But the people who wrote the stories must not have been the ones to live under the king's roof. I could hear Gerroc's gentle jealousy in her voice. She wanted a father like mine.

I, on the other hand, wished for a father like hers, a mild-tempered man who never said an unkind word to his wife or children, and spent his time with his wife and children when he was at home, not striding about the tuath, shouting orders.

On his second day home, my father left his gelding to graze and strode from one house to another, to the fields, then back, exhorting everyone to work harder, faster. The cloth my mother bound his arm with soaked through with blood, then got dirty. He let her change it only in the evening and then groused that he had no time to be coddled. He did not smile at her when she brought his food or thank her, as he had at first.

Within two long days, the fields were plowed—with the men changing to fresh horses and plowmen midday to keep up the pace. Planting began on the third day. It was bruising hard work, I tell you true: We all slept like stones at night and barely crept out come each new morning.

Women and girls cleaned corn and barley and oats for the planters to sow, looking for seeds of darnel or corn cockle that sometimes gets mixed into the harvest. Both are poisonous, so we were very careful.

Women planted their house gardens. It warmed all our spirits to see the fine celeriac seed trickled into the planting stick's tracks and the tiny pebble seeds of the cabbage placed in the soft soil near our houses. Garlic cloves were pressed into the dark earth, too, and leek bulbs were tucked into the mounded beds that let them grow deep, long roots. The women traded seeds and cuttings. They planted herbs for healing and to add flavor to meat and cheese. It made my mouth water to think about all the good foods we would soon have again.

We spent one long afternoon setting out bee houses made of dried clay. We put them in trees with low limbs, in the eaves of the stock byres, and anywhere else we thought might attract a summer swarm. I selected my places very carefully. No one loved eating a dripping honeycomb more than I did. Except Bebinn.

Every corner of my heart was lonely without her. And now I had no soft-muzzled gray mare to tell my troubles to. Every morning I cried, passing the empty rath.

Gerroc and I trudged away at our labor, working with the women after we finished each pitiful milking. Every time I saw Bebinn's mother, my heart ached anew. Her eyes were red day and night from crying. Tally was like a different boy. His high spirits seemed gone forever. The very sky seemed less blue to me.

And yet we worked. We all worked like people in a dream who cannot rest.

Gerroc and I were helping to sort the oats—some of the seed grain had gotten wet over the winter and had rotted. We sat, hunched over a cloth spread on the ground, picking out the blackened kernels.

We had set up on the little slope in front of my father's house. There were several groups doing the same thing, scattered through the meadow, all of us going as fast as we could go.

Fallon was walking a long circle between the groups of seed cleaners, carrying the oat seed down to the fields as we finished. She had taken two or three baskets from us without a word. Then she walked up the hill again to get the last of our cleaned oat seed. "Aunt Orlaith's fingers are aching," Fallon said. "She asks if you two would take the rest of hers to sort."

I glanced up and then down again. "Of course."

"We're finished with what we have," Gerroc said, standing up to stretch. "I can walk down and get it from her."

"I'll go with you," I said. "My legs hurt from sitting so long. We can work down there."

Fallon made a rude little sighing sound, as though we were finding an excuse to play while others worked—which was completely unfair. It made sense for us to walk down the hill to Orlaith's house.

"It won't waste even a little time and it will save a bit, if you think about it, Aunt Fallon," I said in a voice that was sharper than I meant it to be.

"No," Fallon said. "What I think is this: Once you get down there with the rest of the girls, you'll all start giggling and wasting time."

"We are not little children!" I said, before I could stop myself. "We work as hard as anyone."

"My brother might want to know that you are rude to me," Fallon said, which did not surprise me. She always threatened to tell my father whenever anyone did anything she disliked. And he often took her side.

I stared at Fallon's angry face and realized something for the first time in my life. She was so very much like my father. She was entirely sure that she knew how things should be done, who should do them, how the tuath should be organized—but she couldn't give orders and have things her way. Like me, Fallon had been born a girl and would never have the life she wanted.

"Lara wasn't being rude," Gerroc said when the silence went on too long.

Fallon frowned.

"I was a little," I said quickly, wanting peace more than anything. I was too hungry and too tired to want a fight.

I wondered if Fallon had told my father about the ruined comb. Without thinking, I slid my hand beneath the folds of my brat and touched the little gold pin.

I saw Fallon looking at me, her head tilted to one side. I pulled my hand from beneath the woolen cloth and stared off in another direction. The last thing I wanted was for her to wonder what I was hiding.

Without another word, Fallon stalked away, carrying the last few handfuls of our oats. Gerroc and I waited a moment, not wanting to walk right behind her down the slope.

We could hear her muttering, probably complaining to every blade of new spring grass about us taking a few minutes to walk the knots out of our legs and backs against her wishes.

Halfway down the gentle rise, Fallon turned. "Lara!" she shouted.

I am ashamed to say I pretended not to hear her. I kept walking, keeping my eyes on the ground.

"Lara!" she shouted a second time.

I looked up to see her pointing. There, in the distance, just visible, came a girl. She was walking fast but not running, her cloud of orange hair a wild thicket around her head, visible even at this distance. And unmistakable.

Gerroc clutched my arm. "Is that . . . ?" She took a deep breath and held it.

I nodded, my lips trembling, my eyes filling with tears. "It is. Oh, thank all the saints it *is*! Bebbin's coming home to us!" My heart flew and fluttered inside my chest, wild with happiness and relief.

"Let's go tell her mother!" I said, and Gerroc and I set off running, racing past Fallon, breathless with joy. We found Bebinn's mother and my own easily; both of them were planting oats that morning. My mother's face lit with happiness at the news. Bebinn's mother began to weep. While we were all hugging one another, Fallon caught up with us. She stood watching, with her arms folded, as Bebinn's mother wiped at her eyes.

"Where is she?" Bebinn's mother pleaded, shading her eyes and looking in every direction but the right one. I led her uphill a little ways, then took her shoulders and pointed. "There. See?" I felt her tremble, then her shoulders heaved up and down in a deep breath.

"I'll go meet Bebinn," I told her. "I'll bring her straight here to you."

Fallon cleared her throat and I jerked around, surprised to see her so close. "Finish the oats. Bebinn is not hurt. She will be here soon enough."

Bebinn's mother was silent and I knew why. My father usually stood with Fallon. If he was home, whatever she said won out. We could all hear him shouting in the distance, keeping everyone working hard.

"Let her go," my mother said, coming closer. "Gerroc, too."

Fallon opened her mouth to speak.

My mother lifted one hand. "Hush. Don't you understand anything? Bebinn is coming home. Rejoice. Others can clean the oats."

"Everyone else is busy at their own work," Fallon snapped.

"You aren't," I said.

Her face went deep red. For once, I wasn't scared of her. I knew she would tell my father, and I didn't care. I understood her anger better now, but I had no time for it.

Not today.

Not this happy, joyous, blessed day.

Gerroc and I exchanged a glance, then we ran downhill. I knew the instant Bebinn saw us coming, because she stopped and held out her arms and stood that way until we finally reached her. We stood swaying in the warm spring sunshine, our arms locked, our heads together. I remember thinking that everything would be all right with Bebinn back, that nothing bad would happen for a long, long time.

CHAPTER TEN

❧ ❧ ❧

There was an argument, angry shouting, and some of the men have left. I must go my own way; somehow, I must get away from these men and find a place to rest before my foal comes.

I t was pure joy, having Bebinn home. That first day, her mother simply put her into her bed. Poor Bebinn had wandered for days, dark and light, without a moment's rest. Then she had found our creek and followed it home.

Bebinn rested for a day, then helped us prepare for the Feast of Beltaine. She barely spoke to anyone at first. Then, slowly, she began to make jokes again. She told Gerroc and me that she hadn't been hurt at all—only scared. I was so glad, so relieved to know that.

We were not having any of Athenry's noble-men as guests—they would spend Beltaine in far fancier surroundings than we could offer. It was fine with us. No one wanted them.

Everyone was in good spirits, though we were all weary. Under my father's relentless goading, the plowing was finished, gardens were planted, all our work caught up.

We had no oats left to make the traditional Beltaine grain soup. Still, my father ordered two pigs killed to roast. Two! That meant there would be enough meat and blood pudding for every-one. Talking and laughing, the men dug a deep pit at sunrise and laid a fire in it, with a layer of stones beneath the wood. They kept the flames high, and the sharp scent of burning oak wood drifted through the tuath.

Mother and I took baskets and walked the edge of the woods until we came upon a fine patch of lamb's-quarters we had never seen before, the new little plants a soft green. "If we didn't need it," my mother said, "I'd leave it to grow and harvest big-ger, and even then I'd leave some to make seed."

She took out her herb knife and began cutting.

I bent down to help. We left one plant in five untouched. On the way back, we found cress and sorrel. The day was fine and warm and my mother sang old songs as we walked.

Fallon's favorite cousin had a basket of apples stored deep in the ground on the shelves of his corroc. They were wrinkled and some had molded stems and cores, but most were edible. My mother and the other women sliced them thin so that everyone got a few bites at least.

My father was the one with the biggest surprise. He left at dawn and came back with a half-dozen wild ducks. The women were overjoyed. The littlest children ran in circles, laughing. Magnus began a round of singing.

So now, on the first day of summer, when we usually had so little to eat that we celebrated quietly with prayers and songs, my father's people had reasons to think he was wonderful. I stood off to one side, watching. I knew that tonight, by our own house hearth, he would be full of angry war talk again, or he would be shouting at me for some small thing. I looked at Gerroc's father. He was not being admired by everyone present, but he had one arm around his daughter's shoulders.

I sighed and looked away, noticing Bebinn talking to Tally. They could not seem to stop smiling at each other and were holding hands. I was so glad to see her happy again, here again, home for good and all. I wondered if I could have been as brave as she was, if I would have had the courage to creep off into the forest alone. Then I tried to end my somber thoughts and to concentrate on the hope Beltaine always brought.

This year, the girls gathered flowers for their hair and the singing and celebrating went on half the night. Our Beltaine meal might have been taken from pigs we should have kept for wintertime, and our boiled greens picked too young from the woods, but our bonfires were *huge*.

My mother says the custom of the fires comes from somewhere backward in the fog of time, long before the Normans, long before even the priests and the abbeys and their saints. Beltaine fires are made big, and smoky. Then we herd the cattle close to the fires to let the smoke wash over them and the firelight dapple their black sides. This protects them against disease and accident, or so said my grandmothers, both of them.

People prayed aloud only to the saints, especially when there were priests near enough to hear. I am sure that many silently asked the old gods and the faeries for help as well. I did. And we still ran the cattle between the fires.

The day after the feast, with the men still tired and some with headaches from the holiday honey mead, we prepared to leave for the high pastures with the cattle. I was still scared, but I was excited, with Bebinn back, to be going up to the high pasture with the cattle. If the gray mare had not been stolen, I would have begged my father to let me take her with us. As it was, I only begged him to keep an eye out for her.

"I will," he said, looking over my head and shouting out an order before he looked at me again. "I will."

I thanked him.

"I have watched you working," he said, suddenly focusing on me. "You aren't lazy."

Praise from my mother made me blush. Praise

from my father stunned me senseless. "Thank you," I stammered.

"Be sure you all take turns keeping watch at night," he said.

I nodded.

"I will send a few men in a fortnight, to bring back whatever cheese and butter you've made." He looked hard at me, then at the sky. I thought he was going to speak again, but he just let out a long breath and walked away.

"We're depending on you," my mother said after he had gone. Then she kissed my forehead.

We had a fair amount to carry. I had already sorted out my load, but I did it again because I was too jittery to stand doing nothing.

Each of us had a linen sack filled with whatever we couldn't leave behind. I was bringing an extra leine—the one that was a little too small now—an old yellow brat of my mother's, and a blanket. We all carried a little food, a tiny portion of whatever our families had left, as well as a separate sack that held what we would need to make cheese. I carried my share of the sheep's-gut rennet and packets of salt and herbs to flavor the cheese.

To eat, we would rely on scant milk, greens from the woods, and whatever we could find until calving began and the cows came back into milk. Then we would start making cheese. The salt and rennet we were carrying would be used up, but visitors from home would bring more, and then take our new-made cheese and butter back to the tuath.

While we worked at the dairy our families would labor in the fields. If the wheat and corn grew well, if the peas and vegetables were kept free of beetles and bugs, soon none of us would be going to bed hungry. It made my mouth water to think of pea porridge—the Beltaine feast had been the first and only generous meal any of us had had in months.

I hefted my sacks, then tied the open ends together to sling them over my shoulder. I was grateful that the cauldrons and pots we would need were already there.

I found myself watching my mother as she talked to Bebinn's mother. They had both taken the cows to high pasture many times as girls. Bebinn and Gerroc kept looking at their mothers, too. I suppose I wasn't the only one who was a little scared as we stood waiting for the herd.

The boys had gone to drive the cattle down the slope, bringing them from their grazing. Dailfind and Inderb, the two older girls who would be guiding us, had gone with them to make sure no animals were left behind. Fallon's uncle would send some of his sheep—the ewes with half-grown lambs. Normally, we would have been taking some of the horses, too. But this year we had none to spare.

My mother and I held each other tightly for a long time. "You will do fine," she whispered. "Fallon is hard-natured, but she will do her share. And I know you will, too."

I stepped back. "Fallon?"

My mother nodded. "Your father insists that she go. He says she can help with any problems."

I did not say what I was thinking: My father was probably sick of her. Having Fallon come with us solved *his* problem. What I said to my mother was this: "I wish you were coming."

She stroked my hair and I closed my eyes. "I will miss you," she said.

"Here they come!" my father shouted.

I saw Bebinn and Gerroc stepping back from their families. I could hear the boys' voices, calling to the cattle, their high clear whistles. There were other voices, too, as everyone joined in, circling the herd to keep them together while we readied ourselves with one last embrace, a few more words of advice. My mother smiled at me and I waved. Then the people on the far end of the circle stepped away. Dailfind and Inderb clapped their hands and came forward, and the cows began to walk. I spotted Fallon, off to one side with the sheep.

This is odd but true: I had never felt stranger in my life than I did walking away from the tuath, waving at my mother until we rounded a curve of the path and I couldn't see her anymore.

Dailfind and Inderb were both seventeen. They were good friends and they began talking the moment we left, ignoring us and Fallon, who stayed off to one side the rest of the day.

Bebinn, Gerroc, and I walked some distance apart, staying a little ways behind the herd, to make sure that no cows wandered off or stopped to graze so long that they were left behind.

It felt odd to me to know that we were on our own. None of the older women had come—which wasn't unusual—but it felt strange to me. And of course, the men and boys had all stayed home.

I glanced at Bebinn and felt silly for being nervous. We would face no danger. We would be two days' walk from home—no more than that. People from the tuath would come soon to get cheese and butter.

I took a deep breath and tried to let my worries go with it when I let it out. The day promised fair. The air was cool and the forest was quiet. Only the sound of the cattle broke the stillness. Gerroc smiled at me and I smiled back.

Dailfind and Inderb had been to the high pasture three times before, so they directed us along, sticking to the flat meadows as the sun rose, then easing the herd one way or another to find easy creek crossings and better grazing as we went. No rí, no tuath, owned the land we were passing through. Anyone who wished to graze animals here had the right. It was the law.

Our cattle were all thin and most were with

calf. So we did not rush them when we came to hock-high stands of fresh grass. Fallon sometimes went ahead a little, but stayed in sight. The ewes balked at every stream we crossed. Each time it took all of us to bring them around and get them running, forcing them to plunge into the water. Once in, they did fine—the water wasn't deep.

I found myself taking deep breaths of oak-scented air when we passed close to the edge of the forest, digging my toes into the warm soil, humming as we walked. Herding cattle is a pleasant, mindless task. So long as they are not scared witless by something, cattle are content to walk and graze—it is their natural life, after all.

That night we camped atop a low hill. We made a simple supper of boiled corn and rock-hard cheese. Fallon camped a little ways off with the sheep backed up against an outcropping so they wouldn't startle and scatter in the night.

Once Dailfind and Inderb had hobbled the lead cows, we settled in and laid out our blankets. Soon they were dozing. Dailfind snored. We began to whisper.

"Bebinn, will you tell us about it someday?" Gerroc asked.

Bebinn shifted, rolling over onto her belly. "About being captured?"

"Yes," Gerroc said. "Were they cruel to you?"

Bebinn sighed. "No. I told you. No one hurt me at all."

"No one even saw them take you," I told her.

Bebinn sat up. "They only meant to take the horses." She folded her hands in her lap. "It was like this. I was standing with one arm flung upward, shouting at my mother to run, just as the man galloped past."

She shuddered and neither Gerroc nor I said a word.

"I think he just saw me, close by like that, and he caught my arm and dragged me up in front of him," she went on. "I fought, but . . ."

Gerroc and I exchanged a look. No girl our age stood a chance at matching the strength of a grown man.

"Once I was up," Bebinn went on, "he reined hard to the side and galloped into the woods. That's why no one saw. He hid. He waited until

the others had our horses running, then he galloped back into the clearing to follow them."

Gerroc let out a long breath. "He didn't hurt
you?"

Bebinn shook her head. "No. Truly. He apol-
ogized to me. But he wouldn't let me go."

"How far did they take you?" I asked.

"They rode hard," Bebinn told us. "All that
day and into the next. At sunrise we were headed
straight into the rising sun."

"Going east, then," Gerroc said. "Normans?"

Bebinn smiled. "No. But Lara's father asked
me that, too."

I blinked. I hadn't known he had talked to her.

"They were Irish," she said. "Not Normans. I
don't know what tuath, what clan. I . . ." Her
voice faded. "The most terrible thing was thinking I would never see you two again, or my
mother and brothers. Or Tally."

She paused, and I could imagine her blushing,
though it was too dark to see. "Then, after the
man was kind to me, I worried about Lara's
father being angry and riding after me, how it
would become a war."

I nodded. That had scared me, too. It still did. If my father raided them, they would probably try to raid us again.

"How did you get away?" Gerroc asked.

Bebinn smiled. "That part was simple. When they finally stopped to camp, I lay there listening to them talk, pretending to sleep. Once all of them were snoring, I crept away. I wanted to bring your gray mare home to you, Lara," she said softly. "But I was afraid the horses would neigh if I led her off. I ran all night and hid when it got light. I doubt they even looked for me. They seemed in a hurry to get home."

I reached out to touch Bebinn's cheek. "Thank you for even thinking of the mare when you were so scared."

She shrugged. "They were like the men of our own tuath. They gave me cheese from their provisions, and water . . . and I don't think they had any more food than we do."

She fell silent then. When she did speak again, her voice was soft and thoughtful. "I heard them talking. None of the men wanted a feud with your father, Lara. They were angry at the man for taking me captive. They had only meant to steal horses to get even for a raid before Imbolc."

I clenched my fists hearing that. "There was more to it than that," I said. "My father would not steal from someone who had done him no wrong."

"Maybe the wrong was ten years ago, though," Gerroc said.

I knew it was possible, and I pressed my lips together.

"They recognized the gray mare," Bebinn said quietly. "They said she belongs to some powerful rí—someone they're afraid of."

"My father found her wandering and wounded," I whispered, wondering now if he had lied, if he had been part of the battle that had wounded her.

"I am only saying what I overheard," Bebinn said quietly.

She paused for a long moment, so long that I thought she was through talking about it. When she did speak, her whisper was barely audible.

"The man who captured me said his wife was going blind from clouded eye and that she needed help in the kitchen," Bebinn said. "They have no daughter and she is scared alone. That's why he wanted me. To help his blind wife."

Gerroc made a little sound of sympathy. Her grandmother had been blind the last ten years of her life. I exhaled slowly, unsure what I was feeling.

"Do you understand now?" Bebinn said. "This is why I haven't talked about it. I hated him for taking me, but I pitied his wife. I was sorry for them all. They lost three old people in the cold of Gam for lack of food—because someone robbed them of most of their horses and they couldn't trade for wheat and rye." She hesitated, then whispered, "I don't want to hate them."

No one said anything as we each sorted through our thoughts. Had my father been the one who raided their tuath? It was possible. He told stories about *how* he fought, not about *why*.

"He will try to find them now, regardless of what went on before," I said quietly. "Even though you are home and safe, he will want to make it even for our mares."

"Even," Bebinn echoed.

I nodded, knowing her thoughts without her

saying them. When would they ever be even?

As we lay in silence, drifting toward sleep, I thought about the gray mare. Wherever the truth about my father lay, the mare had done nothing to deserve being galloped breakneck across rough country with her foal so close to coming.

I listened to Bebinn and Gerroc's breathing deepen as they fell asleep. I dreamed of the mare and her foal—we were back home and my father gave the foal to me. In my dream I cried for joy.

❧ ❧ ❧

I woke to Fallon nudging at me with her foot. "Get up," she said. "Build a fire."

It was still dark. I heard a long, quavery howl and sat up, touching Bebinn's shoulder. "Wolves," I told her. She woke Gerroc.

The cattle were shifting, uneasy, and we heard more howling, first to the north, then to the east as the wolves circled our hill. We were up the rest of the night keeping the fires bright, orange-gold sparks rising into the sky.

CHAPTER ELEVEN

✵ ✵ ✵

The man set to watch us fell asleep, and we all wandered,
looking for better grass. The one who came to find us was
tired, unwilling to walk very far. I stood in the woods,
watching, until he gave up.

*W*e came to the highland dairy byre by midafternoon the next day. We did what all of us knew how to do—we worked hard. Four days later, we were settled, with a new fire pit dug and the dairy byre on the hill crest cleaned out— the mice and spiders gone.

Seven days after that, our first calf was born. The cow had no trouble at all. As if her labor had inspired her acquaintances, there were three more calves born in the next two days. One died, but it was too small and unhealthy looking. Its

mother was young and she seemed sad and lost—
we all felt sorry for her.

Fallon's sheep claimed the north side of the
hill. She milked there, bringing the milk up the
hill in her pails. Later, once our stock had grazed
the area bare, we would have to spend hours finding them new places to eat. But for now, we could
concentrate on making cheese and butter. And
eating. We all drank milk and buttermilk and
even the whey. Our cheeks began to fill in.

Most of Fallon's ewes had older lambs, and
many of them began to nurse less, grazing along-
side their mothers. The ewes who didn't have
lambs hadn't been bred—they were old and being
fattened for the stew pot next fall. One of these
surprised Fallon with a lamb about a week after
the first calf. The lamb was covered with dark
curled-silk hair, and we all held it and patted it
when Fallon was off gathering firewood.

The weather warmed quickly, and as the cows
began to produce more calves and milk, our real
work began. We cleaned out the big stone-lined fire
pits and set up the clabbering cauldrons outside,
where the smoke taste wouldn't cling to the cheese.

Then we washed our cloths in the creek and cleared out the tiny creek byre where we would store butter. Inside it was a pit, filled with seep water from the stream. The cool water would keep the butter solid and sweet.

Milking and cheesemaking are not heavy work compared to cleaning chicken byres or manuring fields or carrying firewood uphill. But it is a constant circle that barely ends when the new day starts at sunset, and begins again with morning light.

First, every morning, we milked. We filled our pails, then the clabbering cauldrons, then the rennet pots. The curds from the days before were rinsed, salted, and pressed.

Salting and pressing goes on longer for hard cheese. We were making mostly soft cheese, for the tuath to eat as soon as it was finished. But soon we would begin making hard cheese, because it lasted longer. Hard or soft, the last step was to form the rounds and wrap them in cloth, then hang them from the rafters to finish.

Now that we weren't half starved, we drank mostly the whey that separated from the curds—

that way the whole milk could all go to cheese. We skimmed the cream each day, and once every four of five days, one of us would churn it into butter. The little byre built beside the creek at the bottom of the hill worked perfectly as a cooling house.

As the days passed, I began to feel like we were floating on an ocean of milk. None of us wanted to waste a single drop. So we worked from dark to dark, some of us tending the cattle, some of us turning summer milk into food that would sustain us until Samhain when we would be able to hunt and eat meat again.

At night, when we were all too tired to talk and the sheep and cattle were dozing, a soft quiet fell over the high meadow. I was usually the last asleep, pestered by my own thoughts longer than the rest. Almost every night I listened to Gerroc and Bebinn's breathing steady and deepen into slumber before I drifted off.

One night, when everyone else was asleep, I heard an odd moaning sound. It didn't scare me. It sounded like a cow, straining to give birth. Few of them needed any help at all, but I knew I should go look. I rose without disturbing anyone else, knowing I could call for help and wake them if I needed to.

There was a half-moon that night, and it touched the grass and the heather with silver. I padded quietly away from my friends, listening intently. The night was silent except for the sound of slumber.

I had to walk a good ways before I heard the sound again. I changed direction, having mis-judged the first time. I slowed, scanning the moonlit ground, looking for a cow with her head up, her belly heaving.

The sound came again, a higher pitch this time. I stopped, my heart pounding. It sounded like a mare. We had no horses with us and we had seen none. A wild horse?

I stopped, listening. After a long time, I heard a low grunt. Convinced that I had imagined the higher pitch and sure there was a cow trying to calve somewhere nearby, I started forward again.

I was past the main herd and was sure I had walked too far when I heard heavy breathing and another low moan. I walked faster. Any cow this far from the smell of humans and cookfires was wolf bait, plain and simple. I would sit with her, ready to shout for help if I heard wolves. When the calf was dry, I'd carry it up the hill and the mother would follow. Once I was close enough, I would call to the others for help.

I heard another groan and I followed the sound, sliding down a steep slope, catching my balance at the bottom. Then I stopped, listening. There was silence for so long that I began to fear the cow had died and that I was too late. I stood rooted, knowing that I couldn't leave until I was sure.

A rustling sound began, off to my right. I followed it, but slowly. As I came around an old, twisted oak, I saw the mare in the moonlight. I would love to tell you that I recognized her instantly, but I did not.

All I could tell was that she was light-colored and that she was in terrible trouble trying to foal. She was lying on her side, her swollen belly jutting upward. I ran across the clearing, then slowed, speaking quietly. Even so, I startled her. She heaved herself half upright, then managed to stand.

"Are you wild?" I asked her, talking a little louder.

She whickered and I felt my heart sink, then rise. It was the gray mare. And she knew me! Without fear now, I approached her, rubbing her cheek and her forehead. She was shaking, exhausted, and still her foal had not been born. Her eyes were dulling and it took all my will to walk to her trembling hindquarters to see if I could tell what was the matter.

As I stood there in the moonlight, she heaved once more, straining hard to push her foal into the world. I felt its muzzle, as was right, but only one small hoof.

"You can do this," I told her, sliding my hands over her back, beneath her mane. She leaned against me. "I missed you so much," I said, without knowing I was going to say it. My eyes flooded with tears.

The mare lowered her head and blew warm breath against my cheek. Then she made a low sound that frightened me. I waited for her next push, and this time I pulled one front hoof free, then reached past it, trying desperately to catch hold of the other one. But I couldn't.

I rubbed the mare's muzzle again, trying to talk strength into her. Trying not to cry, I stood close as she swayed, clearly too tired to stand much longer.

Most mares give birth lying down, but I was afraid that if she went down now, she would give up. The next push was long and her whole body convulsed, her back arching as she strained. I tried again to get the foal into the right position. I touched the other hoof with my fingertips, but could not hold on. I was shaking, furious with myself, knowing I would only get a few more chances before she gave in to her exhaustion and lay down to die—taking the foal with her.

Oh, how I hated the men who had galloped her so hard. I hated them for losing her like this, or more likely, just leaving her behind when she couldn't keep up.

When she groaned again, I worked my hand around the second little hoof and pulled, steady but hard. When the mare sagged, heaving out a long breath, there were two hooves showing, and the foal's tiny muzzle.

Twice more the tired mare heaved. And now that the foal's forelegs were aligned correctly— and with me pulling steadily on them—the baby began to emerge. On the third push, the foal slid into the cool night air.

I caught it in my arms, awkwardly, and staggered a step or two to lower it to the ground. My hands shaking with worry, I cleared the baby's nostrils and knotted the umbilical cord. The foal took a long, jerky breath, then another, slower and deeper.

I ducked out of my brat, removing the little gold pin and fastening it inside the hem of my leine.

Frantic to dry the foal before it was chilled, I worked fast, rubbing its coat. It was a filly, a perfect, long-legged filly, and in the moonlight, her coat shone like silver.

When the foal was dry, I turned back to the mare and saw that what I had been dreading had come true. She had lain down again, and her sides were barely moving. Her breath was quick and shallow, and her eyes were closed.

Crying, I wrapped the foal in my brat and

settled it on the ground, then went to sit beside the gray mare, talking softly to her, stroking her neck, telling her how sorry I was, that I would take care of her foal and would never forget her.

I stayed beside her until she stopped breathing. Then I stood up and stumbled backward, tears running down my face.

"No."

I whispered the word, but I had meant to shout it. This could not be. I had found her. I had helped her birth her foal and the baby was all right —and none of it mattered anymore because there was nothing anyone could do to help her.

I went to the foal and sank to my knees beside it, then lay down, curling myself around the newborn. I inched closer, crying, fitting my chest and belly against its back, laying my arm around its neck.

I closed my eyes, telling myself I would carry the foal up the hill in a minute, after we both rested a little. I felt the little filly relaxing inside my embrace. I heard it sigh. And that is how Bebinn found us just after dawn.

CHAPTER TWELVE

❧ ❧ ❧

I am frightened. But the girl is close by, with her soft voice and gentle hands and her warmth.

"Lara? Are you all right? Lara?"

Even in my sleep I knew Bebinn's voice, and I woke up without being startled or afraid. I half sat up and the foal woke and rolled upright with me, its long front legs arched at the knee, its eyes wide. As my mind came awake, I remembered everything, and I turned to glance at the mare, still and cold. My eyes filled with tears.

"Oh, Lara," Bebinn said as she got closer and saw what had happened. "We were so frightened when we woke up and you were gone, but we never thought . . ." She walked closer. "That's *your* mare, isn't it?"

"Maybe I can carry the filly back home," I said. I was still muddleheaded with sleep, and all I knew was that the foal needed milk. If any good was ever to come out of all this sorrow, I had to save the foal.

"Carry her—" Bebinn began.

"Yes," I said. "If the bay mare still has enough milk, maybe I can get her to nurse the filly and . . ."

I trailed off because it was impossible. The baby needed milk now. In the two or three days it would take me to get home with her, she would die of hunger.

I started to cry again. Bebinn sat beside me. The foal lifted her head, her eyes wide as she stared into my face. I kissed her muzzle and rearranged my brat to keep her warm. Her coat was completely dry now, her color even lighter than I thought.

I wiped at my eyes. The filly extended her muzzle and touched my cheek, inhaling my scent. She was so beautiful. Her legs were dark from the knee down and her muzzle and ears were shaded black. Her mane was dark as midnight beneath an oak, and it grew short and spiky along the curve of her neck.

"Lara! Where are you? Bebinn? Answer me!" It was Fallon. I could hear her heavy footsteps, coming down the hillside. She shouted my name once more and her voice was harsh and shrill.

"We're down here, Fallon," Bebinn called back.

"I don't have time to be chasing you around and making sure that you—" Fallon's eyes went wide as she came around the tree and saw the mare, then the foal. "What a shame," she said.

She half turned, then looked back up the hill. "Both of you, get back up to the dairy byre now. Dailfind and Inderb can barely hold the cattle. There's another tuath's herd at the foot of the hill on the north side."

"Why are they here?" The words were barely out of my mouth before I could stop them.

Fallon scowled at me. "Addlebrain! How would I know why they're here? What I do know is that if the cattle mix, there will be trouble from here to next year. Come on!"

I struggled to my feet with Fallon shouting at

me to leave the foal. When she saw I would not, and that Bebinn would not leave me, she turned and ran back to help with the cattle.

We followed as fast as we could. Bebinn helped me carry the foal. The filly was confused, scared to have her legs dangling, and she squirmed a little. I was so scared that we would drop her and hurt her, but we managed.

As we passed through the herd of cattle, I noticed the sad-eyed heifer that had lost a calf. Her milk had come in. Her udder was bulging. So were all the others. Between my being missing and the strangers near our hill, no one had milked yet.

Bebinn and I set the foal onto her four little hooves, then I held her so she wouldn't fall. Bebinn touched my face. "Stay with her. We'll manage."

"They've gone off," Fallon shouted to us before Bebinn could take a single step. "They saw me and they turned off."

I exhaled, relieved. There were stories about herds mixing, and Fallon was right; it was trouble for good and all. Everyone could pick out the few cows in their herd that looked a tiny bit different from the rest. There were cows with chipped horns, or misshapen hooves, or flecks of white on their coats. But the rest . . . ? When cattle had to be separated, no one thought they had gotten back their own.

Dailfind and Inderb saw the foal and began making their way toward us. I saw Gerroc peek out the byre door. Her eyes went wide, then she ran toward me, with a happy shout. Fallon ignored us all, pacing angrily on the crest of the hill, staring off to the north.

The foal took an unsteady step, and Bebinn and I moved with her. Gerroc ran up, slowing as she got close, breathing hard. Bebinn told her about finding me, about the gray mare.

"The filly is beautiful," Gerroc said sadly. "I wonder if the mare was trying to get home?"

The thought made my eyes sting with fresh tears, but I blinked them back, remembering the sad little heifer whose calf had died aborning.

"She needs a foster mother." I looked at Inderb as she came toward us, then past her at Dailfind. "Have you ever heard of a cow nursing a foal?"

They both shook their heads.

"Leave off worrying over that foal!" Fallon shouted from above. "We have milking to do and cheese to press." When no one moved, she struck her thigh with one fist. "Would you rather play with foals than feed your families?"

Fallon's voice was sharp enough to cut wood, but we all knew she was right. We had to do our work. The tuath—everyone we knew and loved—was depending on us to have as much cheese and butter as possible when they came.

"I can't leave her yet," I pleaded.

"You take care of the filly," Bebinn said. "The rest of us will work harder to make up for it."

They all nodded. Inderb ran the palm of her hand lightly along the soft spikes of the filly's mane. "What an odd color she is."

Dailfind tilted her head. "You'll need a halter."

I nodded. "Two halters. One for the heifer that lost her calf. I brought my old leine and a brat—I'll braid the cloth."

Inderb smiled. "Good idea. I hope it works."

I could feel the filly's heart beating against my chest as I steadied her. "It has to," I said.

CHAPTER THIRTEEN

✵ ✵ ✵

My belly is pinched and aches.
It scares me, to be so hungry.

"*I* know you're half starved," I told the foal, rubbing her tiny muzzle. She tilted her head back to take two of my fingers in her mouth, sucking hard.

"She thinks you're her mother," Bebinn said from behind me. "Here. Inderb said to give you these."

She handed me everyone's spare clothes.

I met her eyes. "Thank you, Bebinn. Thank them for me, too."

She held out the short-bladed iron knife we

used to cut bark to hold the butter pats we made. "I brought this, too, to start the tears and to cut the ends. I wish I could just do it for you. But Fallon—"

"I know," I said. "This is more help than I expected. I'm grateful."

She leaned close to kiss the foal's forehead, then mine. "We haven't milked the heifer and we won't," she said. Then she was gone.

I settled the foal into a nest of spare clothes, keeping aside my outgrown leine and my mother's old yellow linen brat. I would cut up my own clothes for the halters first. Maybe I wouldn't need more.

The braiding took me longer than I wanted. The foal's halter was easy enough—she was small and it didn't need to be stout. I made the one for the heifer thick and strong as I could. I used Bebinn's old leine as well as my own and some of the yellow brat. I only had enough cloth for a short lead, but I wouldn't need a long one.

The foal was asleep, her dark lashes resting on the gray silver of her coat. "Stay here," I whispered when I stood up. I stuck the knife high in a sapling oak so she wouldn't step on it if she woke. I spotted the heifer and took a deep breath, then started off, careful to walk silently until I was a good distance away.

Cows are not trained to be led like horses. The heifer let me put the halter on after a few tries, but she didn't want anything to do with me. I pulled and cajoled and tugged, but she wouldn't follow.

I kept glancing up the hill. Once, Gerroc was there. She waved, then ran back to work. I hoped Fallon hadn't seen her idling. The last thing I needed was for Fallon to turn her perpetual anger on me—or worse yet, the foal.

I finally picked a tempting handful of grass and held it out to the heifer.

Glorious day, it worked!

The cow took a few steps, with me backing up, keeping the tender grass just out of reach. Then she snatched it from me and chewed, planting her hooves again. We repeated the process.

It worked until I was almost to the top of the hill, then she dropped her head to graze on a rich patch of grass, ignoring me completely. I tugged on the lead and she jerked her head, irritated, pulling it out of my hands. I grabbed it back and she sidled away from me, bawling softly. I looked at her udder. It was so full it looked stretched. It probably hurt.

"You aren't going to get milked today," I told her. "But I know a filly who needs a mother as much as you need a calf."

The cow stopped pulling and stared at me, her huge eyes the deep red brown of peat-bog water. I looked uphill and my heart skipped, then pounded. The foal wasn't in the clothes nest.

I turned to tuck the lead rope into the halter so the cow wouldn't step on it until I could get back to her. When I spun around to run uphill, I almost fell over the foal. She whickered and wobbled toward me, reaching for my hand.

My pulse still pounding, holding my breath, I steadied the foal against my leg, then patted the cow's back and flank in a calm, careless way, like any milker does when she sets to work.

The cow stood still.

The foal took another clumsy step.

The cow blinked, looking at the filly. She had

been milked only three or four times and was just getting used to it. Out in the open like this, without a tie post, or a spancel to hobble her, even a calm old cow would be hard to milk. This one was young and she had no idea what to make of me, or the horse-child at her side.

"Stand still," I said firmly, guiding the filly forward. Her instincts would tell her to reach up to nurse—but the heifer was not nearly as tall as her natural mother.

Sliding my hand along the cow's side, I reached for her udder, squeezing a few drops of milk onto my finger. The filly licked the milk eagerly, her tongue warm and soft. The cow lowered her head to graze and I dropped the lead, concentrating on the filly. I drew her closer, gently pushing her head down with one hand while I brought forth a little more milk with the other.

Inch by inch, the foal came closer, following my milky hand, finally taking the milk for herself.

The heifer lifted her head and sighed, turning back to look at the foal. The easing of the ache in her udder was obvious on her face. She worked her tongue in and out, like a cow licking her calf.

I stepped back so she could nuzzle the filly. She curled her lip at the strange scent, but she continued licking the filly's side as she nursed. She looked content. The filly's eager nursing was relieving the pressure in her udder just as human hands did when they milked her. She went back to her grazing.

I sat down in the grass, watching with tears in my eyes. This was the simple truth: If the filly could eat, she would live.

After a time, the heifer walked forward. The foal lifted her head and followed, weaving to keep her balance, reaching down to nurse again when the cow stopped to eat.

I heard a soft whistle and looked up to see Gerroc standing outside the byre looking downhill at me. She threw her hands in the air and danced a silent circle, grinning. Then she ran back inside. I heard the happy voices—and Gerroc hushing them—as they lined up to watch. Then, before Fallon could look up from her sheep milking down the hill and notice, they ran back.

When the foal was full and sleepy, I walked her back to her nest of outgrown clothes. Even though she had nursed from the cow, she seemed to think I was her mother in that regard—that she should stay close to me.

She sank onto the cloth and closed her eyes. After a few minutes, she stretched out, sighed, and fell fast asleep. Giddy, silly, full of joy, I ran to help my friends.

The next morning, Fallon watched the foal nurse, making little sounds of disbelief, then of disapproval. "That foal is barely more than skin and bone—it won't live past a few days. It's a waste of good milk."

I was the only one standing near, and I searched for some answer but couldn't find one. She walked off without saying more. I watched her go.

I will tell you true: I was coming near to plain disgust with her. Unless something made her angry, it held no interest for her at all. I knew my own father was much like her. I thanked the saints and the old gods that my mother was not. She was the one I wanted to be like. I wanted to be guided by what I loved, not what I hated.

The foal straightened her neck and lifted her

head. She was tall for a foal and I leaned toward her, feeling her soft breath on my cheeks. I closed my eyes and knelt so she could explore my face, pushing her muzzle gently into each of my eyes, then the crook of my neck. She licked at my ear, then mouthed the bridge of my nose. I sat back, laughing. She shook herself—nearly falling over—and wobbled back to the cow to nurse again.

I left the halters on both of them, even though there seemed to be little use for either one. If nothing else the white-and-yellow braid made the cow easy to spot in the herd.

The foal slept with me every night, the way we had done her first night on this earth. I curled myself against the curve of her back and she slept soundly, her front legs tucked into her chest, through the silent, starry nights.

For her daytime milk-stupor naps, she lay full out, flat against the ground in the shade. On the third day, I moved her nest of old clothes up to the back side of the byre, where I could hear her when she woke and nickered, calling to me. Every moment that she didn't need me, I worked.

More than anything in the world, I wanted to

keep her for my own. I wanted to train her to let me ride her and I wanted the two of us to race through the woods together. That meant I had to prevent Fallon from telling my father I hadn't worked hard enough.

The filly was hungry five or six times a day. It wasn't long before her flesh thickened and she began to manage her long legs better. One morning, after she had had her fill of milk, she raced me up the path. She won, of course.

Bebinn and Gerroc saw her clattering along, kicking up dust, and they laughed with me when I got to the top. The foal was shy with them, but that morning, she let Bebinn touch her neck before she galloped off, circling to come back to me. That morning was the first time the filly didn't fall sound asleep after nursing. She followed me into the byre. I knew she couldn't stay.

Since Fallon was out with her ewes, I set up my workbench in the shade of a tree beside the byre and pressed curds there. The foal cantered in circles around the tree, leaping and playing for a time—then she went back to her clothes pile and slept.

The next day, Fallon saw the filly playing and I thought it might soften her heart, but it didn't. She watched, frowning. "The first time anyone finds a leaf or a bit of sand grit in the cheese, I will explain to my brother exactly how it got there."

I promised her I was being very careful, but she stalked away as I was speaking, her face flushed. When she was halfway down to her sheep again, she shouted my name. At first I was sure that she had thought of one more insult and was turning to hurl it at me. But she only pointed. North.

I ran to tell the others.

CHAPTER FOURTEEN

❧ ❧ ❧

*My mother is slow. When we race, she cannot keep up. But
in the night, if wolves howl, she moves closer, and I know
she will protect me.*

*I*f Fallon were not Fallon, who knows what
would have happened. She began by shouting
at the strangers, waving them off like they were
badly behaved dogs who had run into her yard.

I ran for the byre and took out four pails full
of milk so the filly couldn't spill them—the
wrapped cheese was all safe, hanging from the
roof poles.

Then I closed the filly inside. She whinnied
piteously, but I had to keep her safe, and milling
cattle were dangerous.

Bebinn and I threw dirt on the fires so that if the cattle started to mill, none would stumble into the pits and get burned. Then we sprinted down to the herd. I spotted the braided halter easily and I walked to that side. All the cows were important, but to me, that heifer was the most important cow there would ever be.

"Begone!" Fallon was screaming. "Do you not hear well? Get you gone!"

There were shouts in response.

Everyone had scattered to locate the cattle and sheep, and the four of us drove them slowly, gently, into a loose bunch.

Fallon was still shouting.

"Maybe one of us should go talk to them," Dailfind called to me across the black backs of the restless cows.

I nodded, thinking she meant she would go. But she just stood looking at me.

Bebinn was nodding. "You should, Lara. Fallon is going to *make* them want trouble."

"I don't think she will listen to me," I answered, looking at Dailfind, then at Inderb. "You're both older than she is."

Gerroc frowned at me. "But you are the daughter of our rí."

If I had been a boy, I would have thought of that, I suppose. The son of the rí is always regarded as the one to lead if his father is not present. But I wasn't a boy and I had no idea what to do. All I wanted was to run to the dairy byre and let my silver filly out and comfort her so she wouldn't be afraid.

A fresh round of shouting made me twist around, trying to see over the crest of the hill. I couldn't.

"Try, Lara," Bebinn said. "Tell them who you are and see if you can settle things!"

I swallowed hard and turned toward the voices. I walked fast, trying to think of what I could say that would matter to anyone.

"Get back!"

Fallon was still shouting.

There were several answers, boys' voices. Boys? Summer pasture was usually a job for girls. Something prickled at my thoughts. Were these the raiders who had taken our horses? Had they lost the gray mare close by and come back for her?

I crested the hill and couldn't help glancing back at the byre. The door was still shut fast. Below me, the hillside was dotted with cattle and people, all of them staring at Fallon.

"I am the daughter of our rí," I said, and not a single soul heard me.

Fallon shouted a truly vile insult, and one of the boys, sick of her screaming, picked up a rock and flung it over her head.

"I am the daughter," I began again, raising my voice, but Fallon picked up a stone and threw it, hard. It struck in front of the boy and he flinched, stepping backward. His friends laughed at him. Fallon bent over, looking for another rock.

"I AM THE DAUGHTER OF OUR RÍ!" I roared. Fallon straightened and glared at me. A few of the boys pried their eyes from Fallon to look at me.

"This has been our summer pasture since the rocks began keeping time," I said. One of the boys laughed at the old expression. He was half grown. I looked at the rest of them. A few were older than Fallon. Some looked twenty or more.

"We need to graze our cows a few days before we go on," a man called back.

Hearing a man's voice startled me. Who were these people who sent their boys and men to do what was usually the work of girls? He stepped forward. He was tall and his hair was dark and curled close to his head.

"Do us the courtesy of keeping them close," I called. "Don't let them come up the hill."

The man stepped forward and gave me a little bow. "Agreed, daughter of the rí."

No one laughed.

I nodded. I was shaking with fury when I turned to walk toward Fallon. She stared at me as I got closer.

"Fallon," I said when I knew she could hear me clearly. "Please come back to the byre."

She started to answer, but I kept walking, thinking she had to follow me to respond. She might have. I think she was turning to come with me when the stone hit her from behind.

She whirled around, scooping up a fist-size stone, hurling it down the mountainside. A boy with wild red hair that reminded me of Bebinn's pitched sideways and lay still on the ground.

There was a terrible moment of silence, then a roar of fury from many throats. I looked at the realization of horror on Fallon's face, then I ran.

"Get the cattle moving," I shouted at Bebinn and the others. "Fallon threw a stone. The boy is hurt or dead!"

Bebinn shouted something back, but I veered for the byre and didn't hear. The filly was shaking as I pulled her into the sunshine, her eyes rimmed in white, her neck arched. I led her as fast as I could over the crest of the hill, then downward, toward the herd of cows. The girls already had them moving more or less in one direction.

I spotted the heifer wearing my braided yellow-and-white halter and followed her. I knew I was not going to be able to run with the others if it came to that, because I was too afraid of the filly getting away from me and getting trampled in the herd.

But I needed that cow.

I tried to walk faster, keeping the filly to a trot, one arm over her neck. The cattle were bawling, uneasy. Behind us, there were shouts, but I couldn't tell if they were getting closer.

The filly whinnied, and her high, shrill voice carried over the din. I saw the cow turn. The filly nickered again. The cow stopped, and my heart leaped. Walking fast, but not faster than the filly could keep up with without breaking into a canter, I wove us a path through the cattle.

I could see Bebinn and the others running as the cows began to trot. They had no idea what was wrong, but they could sense danger and they wanted to get away from it.

I slowed a little, glancing backward. I saw a man walking along the edge of our hill. I tried to imagine what he could see from there . . . the last of the herd disappearing in front of me, a girl, a foal, and a cow, struggling to keep up.

I had no time to ponder because the sound of hoofbeats behind me made me turn.

"Daughter of the rí," a man shouted, and I turned to see him, his dark, curling hair ruffled by wind as his horse galloped along the base of the hill. He reined in toward me. Other riders followed him.

I stopped and stood still. What else could I do? As I turned to face him, I saw Fallon, her hands tied in front of her, the horse she was on being led by a man who rode beside her.

"Daughter of the rí!" the dark-haired man called again. "Did you happen to find a gray mare in the woods? Where is she?"

I looked straight into his hateful eyes. "Dead. You killed her."

He stared, then I saw him make sudden sense out of the way the foal stood half behind me and the protective angle of the cow's stance. He laughed. Then he motioned at one of his men. "Get her up on a horse and put the foal across someone's saddle pad. And bring that cow. It's the nursemaid."

When he looked at me again, he was smiling. "You have no idea how much trouble you have prevented, saving that foal. I want you to be my guest; I have no wish to hurt you. You will be the one to take care of the filly. Will you come willingly?"

There was no doubt in my mind that he wanted the filly, and he was afraid that without me, she might not make it. I was very sure he had no other need of a guest.

I counted the men and boys. There were upward of twenty, all mounted. I had no chance of escape, not here or now. "I will," I said, "if you give me your word that you won't pursue anyone." I gestured in the direction the others had gone.

"Done," he answered, and I could not tell if he was lying. There was little I could do about it, either way.

I was sure of three things.

I would need to be as brave as Bebinn had been.

I would take care of my filly and bide my time.

And one fine morning, they would wake to find us gone.

GAYLORD RG